ACOLTYE

BOUND BY BLOOD BOOK 2

ALSO BY RICHARD FIERCE

DRAGON RIDERS OF OSNEN

Trial by Sorcery
A Bond of Flame
The Warrior's Call
The Coin of Souls
Wings of Terror
Eyes of Stone
Tooth and Claw
The Servant of Souls
Smoke and Shadow
The Dark Rider
The Song of Bones
Sword and Crown
Tides of Darkness
Wrath and Ruin
Tomb of Oaths

MARKED BY THE DRAGON

Curse of the Dragon
Scale of the Dragon
Egg of the Dragon
Call of the Dragon
Wrath of the Dragon
Sacrifice of the Dragon

ACOLTYE

BOUND BY BLOOD BOOK 2

RICHARD FIERCE

Dragonfire Press

Print ISBN: 978-1-958354-97-1

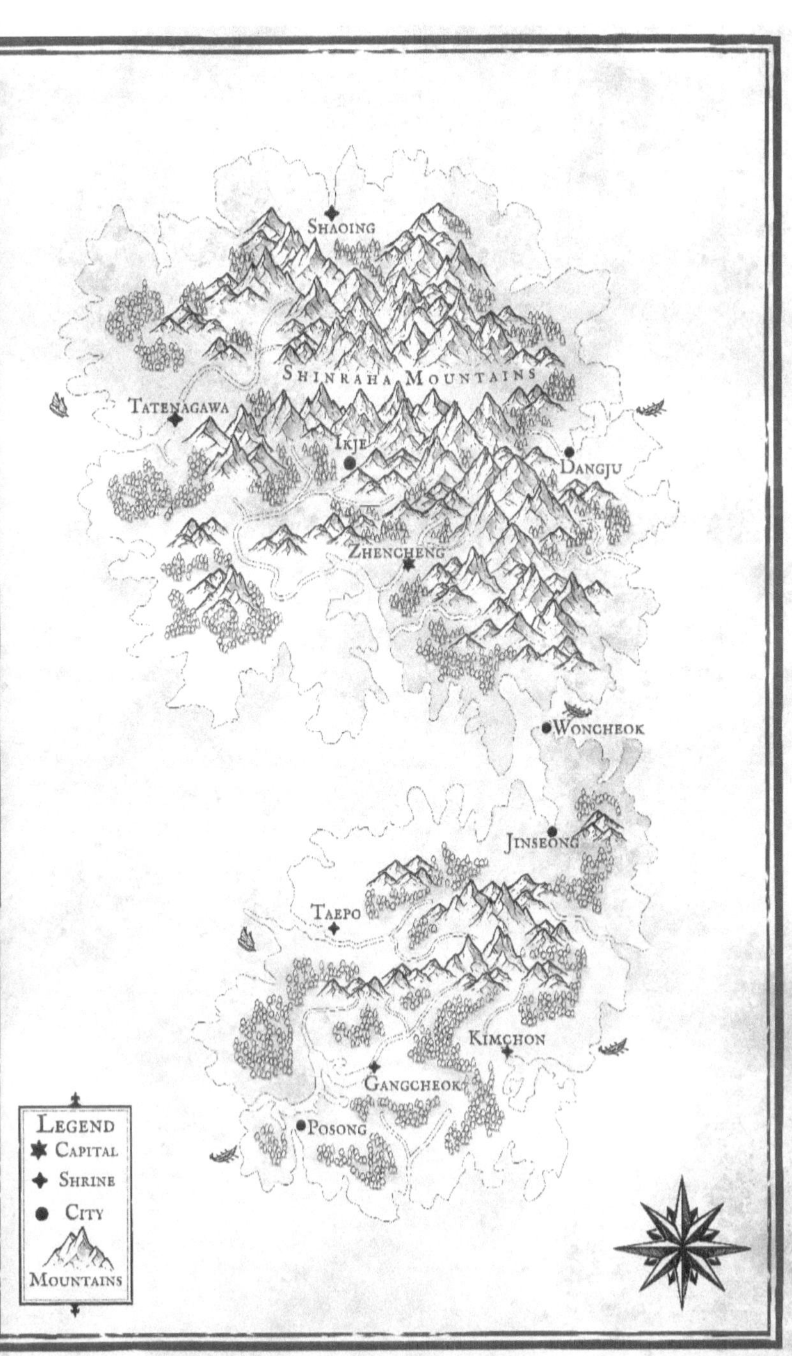

Shaoing
Shinraha Mountains
Tatenagawa
Ikje
Dangju
Zhencheng
Woncheok
Jinseong
Taepo
Kimchon
Gangcheok
Posong
Legend
Capital
Shrine
City
Mountains

CHAPTER 1

Kai walked in the shadows of the great statues that loomed around the temple courtyard—dragons with furled wings and riders whose eyes were fixed on the horizon, seeing things that were lost to time. A gust of wind stirred the dust on the cobblestones, carrying with it the faint scent of smoke.

Ahead, Liu waited for her. His posture was relaxed but alert, and his sword hung loosely in his hand, the blade glinting in the early morning light of the sun. Kai could see the calmness in his eyes, the patience of a warrior who had seen countless battles. She drew her blade, and the metal sang as it came free of the scabbard, the sound sharp and clear in the stillness.

"Ready?" Liu asked. His tone was soft, but there was a hint of something more, an edge that told her this would not be an easy session. Kai nodded, mirroring his stance.

He moved first, a swift, fluid motion that brought his sword arcing toward her with precision. Kai met the strike with her own blade, the clash of metal ringing out through the courtyard. The impact reverberated up Kai's arm, but she held firm, pushing back against Liu's strength.

They moved in a dance of steel, each strike and parry a show of skill. Liu was faster, more experienced, but Kai had her owns strengths. She was learning to anticipate his moves, to read the subtle shifts in his stance that signaled his next attack.

"Very good," Liu said. "Don't just react. Think ahead. Where will my next strike come from?"

Kai tightened her grip on the hilt of her sword. She saw the flicker in Liu's eyes, the slight shift of his weight, and she moved, bringing her sword up to block his next strike.

Their blades locked, and for a moment, they were face to face.

"Better, but you're still focusing on defense. Take the initiative." Liu pushed her back with a forceful shove.

Kai took a deep breath, forcing her anger down. She shifted her position, her eyes searching for an opening. Liu was right. She was too reactive, too cautious. She needed to take control, to direct the pace of the fight. Feigning a strike to Liu's left, he moved to block her, but she shifted her weight, bringing her blade around in a sweeping arc toward his right. Liu's eyes widened slightly in surprise, but he recovered quickly, parrying the blow.

"You're learning well," he said with approval.

Kai didn't let the compliment distract her. She pressed the attack, her strikes coming faster, more aggressively. Liu's blade met each one, but Kai could see she was pushing him now, forcing him to adjust.

They moved across the courtyard, their swords flashing, the clang of metal resonating off the temple. Kai could feel the strain in her muscles, the burn of exertion, but she pushed through it, driven by the desire to prove herself.

Liu's expression remained unreadable, but there was something in his eyes—pride, perhaps, or respect. It was hard to tell, but it gave her the strength to keep going, to push herself even harder.

Finally, Liu stepped back, lowering his blade. Kai hesitated, her chest heaving with exertion, but she lowered her blade as well, sensing the sparring session had come to an end.

"You're improving," Liu said. "But remember, Drakka are formidable enemies, and strength alone won't win you battles. They will outmatch you every time. You need to outsmart and outmaneuver your opponent. Above all, trust your instincts."

Kai nodded, wiping the sweat from her brow with the back of her right hand. She knew he was right. There was still so much to learn, but each session with him brought her closer to mastering the skills she needed to be Sworn. With Liu teaching her to fight, and

Kokoro guiding her in the strengthening of her bond, she knew she would be ready when the time came.

Sensing a shift in the air, Kai turned to see Kokoro. She walked with measured steps and joined them. Liu bowed his head in respect and stepped away. Although Kokoro took the form of a human, Kai couldn't deny her presence was undeniably draconic, and the power she radiated was palpable.

"I see your improvement with each day," she said, nodding at Kai's sword.

"This is easy to navigate," Kai replied. "The bond less so."

"The bond is like a muscle. The more you exercise it, the stronger it becomes. Have you heard her voice yet?"

"No, but I've felt something. Emotions that aren't mine, but they're fleeting. I haven't been able to truly hear her thoughts."

"That is the beginning," Kokoro said, her tone reassuring. "The bond is still fresh, but you have already progressed further than I expected. It won't be long now before she speaks to you. Go bathe yourself and meet me here when you are done."

Kai sheathed her blade and bowed her head, then entered the temple and went to the bathing chamber. The warm water cleansed her body, but her mind was consumed with thoughts of her dragon. If Kokoro was right, she would hear her dragon's voice any day now. Still, doubts lingered. After spending her entire life not hearing the dragon that had originally chosen her, it was hard to believe that her experience now would be any different.

She emerged from the bath feeling refreshed. After drying and clothing herself, she returned to the courtyard where Kokoro waited. Kai's dragon was there, too, and her golden scales shimmered in the sunlight. With each breath, puffs of steam escaped her nostrils, curling and dissipating into the morning air.

"Today we are going to try something different," Kokoro said. "Close your eyes."

Kai obeyed, and she traced her fingers along the material of her pants, searching for a seam to run under her nails.

"Stop that," Kokoro said. "Quiet your mind and focus on your connection to your dragon. Do not force it. Let it come to you naturally."

Kai inhaled a deep breath and pushed all her thoughts aside. She imagined her bond as a thread of light, gold like her dragon's scales. It pulsed with life and energy. For a long moment, there was nothing but silence.

Then, she felt it—a gentle nudge at the edge of her consciousness, like a whisper carried on the wind. It was faint, almost imperceptible, but it was there. Kai's heart quickened as her dragon chirruped, but she forced herself to stay calm.

There was no voice, but there was a presence. A feeling washed over her, more powerful than any spoken language. Kai's breath caught in her throat. She'd not felt her dragon's spirit so clearly before. It was as though a door had been opened between them, allowing them to step into a place where their thoughts could meet.

Kai reached out hesitantly. The response came almost immediately, a wave of warmth that filled her with a sense of peace. She felt the true essence of her dragon; noble, fierce, strong. A rush of raw emotions flooded her mind: pride, love, determination, all amplified by the bond. It was overwhelming, but it was also beautiful. An unspoken word came to her, and she slowly opened her eyes to see Kokoro watching her intently.

"My dragon's name is Hikari."

CHAPTER 2

Hikari.

It meant light, which Kai found fitting considering how her scales seemed to glow.

"A beautiful name," Kokoro said, glancing at the dragon. "Your connection is growing stronger, but it is still a fragile thing. To forge it into something unbreakable, you must face trials that challenge each of you, both physically and mentally."

"What sort of challenges?"

Kokoro's eyes turned skyward for a moment before settling back on Kai. "The skies are the domain of dragons. To truly understand Hikari, to trust in your bond, you must take to the air together. You must learn to fly as one."

The words sent a jolt of fear through Kai's chest. Flying, something she had always admired from the ground, was frightening. She had flown on the back of Siran's dragon to come to the temple, but that was a dragon with years of experience riding the skies. Hikari was practically a hatchling.

"I sense your fear," Kokoro said. "It is a natural response for humans, but it is one you must master."

"What if I can't... what if I fall?"

"You are not alone in this. Hikari will be with you. You will need to trust in her just as she will need to trust in you."

Kai felt a steadying presence wrap around her mind. Hikari's confidence flowed into her, pushing the fear aside. Kai nodded, inhaling a deep breath.

"I will guide you through this," Kokoro said.

Hikari lowered her massive body to the ground to allow Kai to climb onto her back. With trembling hands, Kai approached, running her fingers over the dragon's smooth scales. She could feel the dragon's strength beneath her touch, a living, breathing force of nature that she was now linked to. Kai hoisted herself onto Hikari's back and settled into place at the base of her neck, just ahead of her shoulders.

The fear was still present, but it was overshadowed by Hikari's confidence. The dragon spread her wings wide, their span casting shadows on the cobblestones. With a powerful beat, she lifted off the ground, and Kai watched the earth fall away from her. For a brief moment, panic made her stomach twist, but it was quickly smothered by the exhilaration that surged through her as they soared higher into the sky.

The wind whipped, tugging at her clothes and hair, but she barely noticed. Her entire being was focused on the sensation of flight— the rhythm of Hikari's wings, the rise and fall of their movements, the way the world below grew smaller and smaller until it was nothing but a patchwork of green and brown.

Kai's heart raced, but not from fear. The sky stretched out before them, an open expanse of possibility, and for the first time, she felt a sense of freedom she had never experienced before. She couldn't help but laugh. Focusing her thoughts on the bond, she sent words through it.

This is amazing. I never thought I could feel like this.

The bond hummed with harmony, and Kai knew that Hikari shared her feelings.

The world around them blurred as they entered the clouds, but they parted to reveal the vast blue above. Tears pricked at Kai's eyes, both from the sting of the cold and the pure, unfiltered emotions she felt. This was what it meant to be bonded to a dragon, to share not only thoughts and feelings, but experiences, to face the unknown together.

An unfamiliar voice touched Kai's mind, but she soon realized it was Kokoro.

It is easy to fly in clear skies, but you must be prepared for the worst. Look southeast, toward the mountains.

Kai turned her head, and her eyes widened. Dark clouds swirled ominously, and lightning flickered within them, casting brief, jagged illuminations across the mountain peaks.

I see a storm, Kai said.

The bond is tempered with adversity. Fly through the storm.

The thought of flying into such dangerous conditions brought her forgotten fear back to the surface.

But we've only just flown together for the first time. What if...

What if you succeed? What if you learn to trust in your bond even when the world around you is in chaos? This is not about mastering flight in calm skies. This is about learning to trust one another.

Kai swallowed hard, her throat dry. She knew she needed to strengthen the bond, but flying into a storm seemed a treacherous way to do so. Hikari's presence filled her mind again, calming her.

You are right, she told Hikari. *We can do this.*

Hikari circled around and headed directly for the storm. The air grew cooler as they approached the dark clouds, and the first gusts of wind hit them like a wall. Hikari's wings strained against the turbulence, and Kai could feel the tension in the dragon's muscles. She let out a mighty roar, fighting to keep herself on course as the wind threatened to throw them sideways.

The scent of rain and ozone was sharp in Kai's nostrils. Lightning flashed around them, followed by the deafening crack of thunder. Kai tightened her grip around Hikari's neck, but it was too thick for her arms to fully encircle. She closed her eyes and reached through the bond with her mind, trying to feel what Hikari was feeling—the currents of the wind, the shift of the air pressure, the instinctive adjustments the dragon made to stay aloft. Slowly, she began to sync with Hikari's rhythm, letting the dragon's instincts guide them through the storm.

They dodged several lightning strikes as Hikari banked sharply to avoid the dangerous currents that could send them spiraling out of control. Kai was still afraid, but the emotion was muted by her growing trust in Hikari. She could feel the dragon's confidence, her strength, and it bolstered her own. Feeling brave, she opened her eyes.

Suddenly, a powerful gust of wind caught them from below, lifting them higher than Kai had expected. For a terrifying moment, she felt weightless, the sensation of falling upward sending a jolt of panic through her. Before she could fully process what was happening, Hikari tucked her wings in and plunged downward, cutting through the wind like a blade. The speed was breathtaking, the air rushing past them in a roar. Kai's heart hammered in her chest, but she held on, trusting completely in Hikari's judgement.

The dive took them out of the worst of the storm and into a pocket of calmer air. Hikari flared her wings, slowing their descent just as another bolt of lightning streaked across the sky, narrowly missing them. Kai gasped, temporarily blinded from the flash of light.

After what felt like an eternity, the storm began to break. The clouds thinned, and the rain lessened, revealing patches of clear sky. Hikari's wing beats grew steadier, the turbulence easing as they left the worst of the storm behind. Kai could hardly believe they'd survived.

We did it, she said through the bond, feeling a deep sense of accomplishment. Hikari gave a triumphant roar in reply. As they flew back toward the temple, the sun peeked out from the clouds, casting a golden light over the mountains. The experience had changed something within Kai. She could feel it, a tangible difference in the bond. It was stronger, their connection more intimate.

When they landed in the courtyard, Kai slid off Hikari's back, her legs shaky. Kokoro smiled at her.

"You faced the storm and came out stronger for it. This is the essence of the bond between rider and dragon. It is not without fear, but it is through facing that fear together that you find true strength."

Kai bowed her head. "I understand now. It wasn't just about flying, it was about trusting

Hikari, even when it seemed impossible. Forgive me for questioning you."

Kokoro laid a hand on Kai's shoulder, her touch warm. "There is no need to apologize. You are learning, and to learn, one must ask questions."

Hikari nuzzled Kai, and a wave of affection passed between them.

"Get something to eat and take a moment to recuperate. Your next trial awaits."

CHAPTER 3

"You must seek out an artifact from ancient times. It is imbued with magic that has long since faded from this world. It is known as the Heart of Flame, and it rests in the heart of fire itself."

Kokoro's words echoed in Kai's mind as she sat upon Hikari's back, watching the landscape pass below. Trees and winding rivers slowly gave way to rugged terrain as they approached a mountain with its peak shrouded in a veil of smoke.

A volcano.

Hikari descended, landing at the base of the mountain where the earth radiated warmth, a harbinger of the inferno that awaited them within. A cavernous maw was open to the world, a passage carved into the mountainside by powerful forces, though whether natural or magical, Kai didn't know.

She dismounted and glanced around. The place was so foreboding, she doubted even the Drakka dared to tread here. The opening was wide enough even for Hikari's girth, and Kai was thankful she wouldn't have to brave the dangers of the cave alone.

"Are you ready?" she asked, running a hand along Hikari's scales.

In response, the dragon stared at her with a knowing gaze, then walked into the darkness. Kai cast a final glance at the sky and followed after Hikari. The air inside the cave was heavy and sulfurous, and Kai's lungs protested the oppressive heat that enveloped her. Hikari's massive silhouette was a reassuring presence against the gloom.

The cavern seemed to pulse with the heartbeat of the earth, a rhythmic thudding that matched her own racing heart. Each step took them deeper into the bowels of the volcano, and since Kai was blind in the dark, she was forced to rely on Hikari to guide her.

She held onto the tip of her tail, stepping slowly and cautiously lest she slip on some unseen rock.

Beads of sweat formed on her brow, trickling down her temples, and her clothes clung to her skin. The heat was sapping her strength and clouding her focus. Kai stopped to rest and leaned against the wall. Hikari halted, and a wave of strength flowed through the bond, reinvigorating Kai.

She sent her appreciation to the dragon. There was no need for words; their bond transcended language. Pushing off the wall, she grabbed hold of Hikari's tail again and the two continued ahead. Kai wondered if the riders of old had faced similar challenges. Images flashed in her mind, but they weren't quite memories. The scenes were disjointed and confusing, but Kai was able to discern what Hikari was sending her were echoes of the past, moments lost in time that answered her question.

Yes, the riders of old had faced challenges, but ones much more difficult than she faced now. It was hard to take comfort in that when she felt as though she were suffocating.

A tremor ran through the earth beneath her boots, a murmur from the depths that set her heart racing. Somehow, she could discern the warning: the chamber they sought might soon become their grave. With the urgency of the mountain's message pulsing through her veins, Kai urged Hikari to quicken her pace.

The cavern around them slowly expanded, and the path coiled like a serpent, abruptly ending at an enormous pool of molten rock. The heat was far more intense here, and the air was so acrid it stung Kai's nostrils and made her eyes water. She blinked the tears away and noticed a trail of exposed stones that jutted up from the magma. On the other side of the pool, a luminous beacon flared in the shadows, revealing the entrance to a secondary chamber.

Kai had no doubts the beacon was the relic. Its magic called to her, a beckoning siren song that promised both glory and ruin. Hikari leaped into the air and spread her wings, gliding across the pool and landing on the other side. It was obvious the dragon expected her to navigate across on her own.

The relentless heat tested the limits of her endurance, but she forced herself to press on. She jumped onto the first stone, waving her arms wildly to help her stay balanced. The other stones were spaced closer together, and she nimbly moved across them. Every movement was a dance with danger, but she crossed the magma without incident. By the time she was safely on the other side, her breaths came in sharp gasps, the air searing her lungs as if it conspired with the molten rock to burn away her resolve.

Sweat dripped freely down her face and in places she never imagined possible, but she'd made it, and the chamber was just ahead. An aura of heat intensified with every step until she had to stop and fall back.

"I can't," she hissed. "It's too much."

Hikari sent images through the bond. They flashed vividly in Kai's mind, but they didn't make any sense to her. She wanted nothing more than to lie down and rest.

Hikari growled and more images came to her mind.

"I don't understand..."

The dragon turned her gaze directly on Kai, their eyes locking. Another image came to her, and understanding dawned on Kai. She closed her eyes and focused on the bond. The single golden thread was crafted of many smaller threads, all woven together. Kai found the one in the image Hikari had showed her, and she touched it with her mind.

A magical shield spiraled into existence around her, a cocoon spun from the threads of their intertwined spirits. The barrier shimmered faintly with blue light, repelling the heat. Kai was still sweaty, but at least now she could breathe.

"Thank you. I owe you my life."

Hikari snorted and shook her head. Kai smiled, then looked at the entrance of the chamber. Together, they stepped inside. In the center of the space was a pedestal hewn from the rock, and lying atop it was an object that bathed the entire chamber in a crimson hue. It was a gemstone the size of Kai's fist, and the pulsing she felt in the air was coming from it.

Tentatively, Kai approached and extended a hand toward the relic. The moment her fingertips grazed its sparkling surface, her protective barrier winked out of existence, but instead of feeling the heat return, nothing changed.

The chamber began to tremble, and cracks spiderwebbed across the stone walls. It was as though the mountain rumbled at the disturbance of its treasure. Dust and small stones cascaded from the ceiling, and Kai sensed the earth was warning her to flee.

"Run!"

Turning on her heels, she sprinted out of the chamber, deftly crossing the pool of magma. She reached the other side and continued through the tunnel, the gemstone lighting the way. Hikari was right behind her, the dragon's footfalls echoing like thunderclaps in the hollow cavern.

The path turned treacherous as molten rock oozed from fissures that opened, a glowing menace that hissed and popped. Kai weaved between the obstacles, her agility tested by the earth's convulsions.

Her muscles screamed, yet she dared not slow her pace. Each stride took her closer to safety and away from the destructive embrace of the mountain that sought to reclaim its treasure. The ground heaved beneath her, and the sound of stone cracking reverberated throughout the corridor.

With a deafening crash, the path behind her gave way, succumbing to the mountain's wrath. A torrent of rocks and dust billowed into the air as Kai reached the threshold of the volcano's maw. She stumbled forward, propelled by the force of the eruption and Hikari's bulk. Her boots found solace on the firm soil beyond the reach of the inferno, and she turned back to see the passage was now a smoldering crater. The path was no more, entombed beneath layers of rock and dirt.

"Are you all right?" Kai asked, looking over Hikari with concern. Their bond burned fiercely, and her eyes widened when Hikari replied.

I am now.

CHAPTER 4

High above the clouds, the air was crisp and the horizon stretched endlessly. Kai enjoyed the cooler temperature, thankful that she and Hikari had escaped the volcano unscathed. She had tucked the Heart of Flame protectively inside the silk bag Kokoro had given her, and it rested firmly between her thighs while her hands gripped the scales of Hikari's neck.

The dragon's golden scales reflected the sun's light, casting a faint rainbow of color onto the surrounding clouds. When Kai was younger, she had often wondered what riding on the back of a dragon would feel like. It was better than anything she had imagined, but hearing Hikari's voice was the ultimate reward.

How were you able to show me those images? Are they memories?

I think they are, Hikari replied.

What do you mean? You don't know for certain?

No. They came to me by instinct, and I funneled them to you. I think they are memories from other elders.

Kai found that intriguing. How would a dragon receive memories from another, especially ones that were no longer around? She had many questions, but she feared she would overwhelm Hikari if she let them pour out unchecked.

As our bond strengthens, so do I, the dragon said, answering the main question burning in Kai's mind.

You can read my thoughts?

I can.

That made Kai a little uneasy. Did that mean she would never have privacy within her own mind?

I will not do it any longer without your permission, but you will need to learn to shield your mind from our bond.

Like you, I am still learning, Kai replied.

The wind changed direction, and the smell of smoke was overpowering. Kai leaned to the left, looking down at the ground below.

I smell it, too, Hikari said. *I hear screams.*

Can you reach Kokoro?

There was a moment of silence before Hikari answered, *No. I don't know how to link to her mind.*

Kai could faintly make out a village near the Tangsho river. Smoke billowed into the air, and she knew something was amiss.

We have to help them, Kai said. *Can you take me down there?*

The bond flooded with a mix of concern and pride. Kai thought Hikari would refuse, but the dragon responded with a surge of acceleration and dove, descending toward the village with the swiftness of an arrow. As they got closer, Kai could see the extent of the damage.

Thatched roofs succumbed to hungry flames. The roar of the fire mingled with the cries of the terrified villagers who were running in all directions. Hikari landed on the outskirts of the village, and Kai slid off her back, immediately running to the closest group of people.

"What happened here?"

A woman turned to face her, soot and tears streaking her face. "Drakka," she said. "They came out of nowhere."

Kai glanced around, suddenly afraid. She returned to Hikari and tied the silk bag around the dragon's neck, then drew her ebony blade.

"Go south," Kai instructed the villagers. "Cross the river and turn southwest to Tatenagawa. You'll be safe at the temple."

The small group fled past them, and Kai turned her attention to the village.

Keep watch for the Drakka, she told Hikari. *I'll get the other villagers.*

Without waiting for an answer, Kai hurried across the field and into the village proper. The heat from the flames was intense and threatened to singe her skin. She shouted for people to follow her, directing them toward the river. The acrid smoke filled her nostrils and stung her eyes, but she pressed on, determined to save as many as she could.

As she came around a bend, Kai froze. Several bodies lay in the dirt, but they hadn't been killed from the fire. Blood stained the earth beneath them, and judging by the footprints, they had been victims of a Drakka. Tightening her grip on the hilt of her blade, she cautiously continued ahead.

Sensing movement to her left, she whirled around, bringing her blade up and taking a defensive stance. Through the haze of smoke, a young boy appeared, coughing and gasping for air. His eyes widened at the sight of Kai's sword, but she held out a reassuring hand.

"I'm here to help. Come with me."

The boy accepted her offer and clung to her arm. She led him back the way she'd came, but a Drakka emerged from behind a partially collapsed building. It was similar in appearance to the one she'd seen at Ikje, but this one had red skin.

"Fire," she muttered to herself, realizing what had caused the flames. The Drakka spotted her, and a sinister grin spread across its face. Kai pushed the boy behind her and braced herself, focusing on the rhythm of her breathing. She'd sparred with Liu many times over the last few days, and although she had learned much, she knew she was not prepared to face a Drakka on her own.

The creature lunged at her, claws outstretched, but Kai deftly slapped its arm aside with her blade. The Drakka howled in pain and clutched its arm. Tendrils of smoke drifted off its flesh where her blade had touched it. She hadn't seen it do that before, but she only trained with Liu.

Your sword was forged to destroy Drakka, Hikari said. *I can sense the magic imbued within its metal. It hungers for their blood.*

Emboldened by her dragon's words, she attacked. Her blade struck true and cut a jagged zig-zag up the Drakka's forearm. Black blood oozed from the wound. The creature screeched in anger and struck Kai with its fist. The blow knocked her off her feet, sending her tumbling along the debris-strewn path. Kai landed hard and gasped for breath as pain shot through her side.

Get up, Hikari urged.

Kai struggled to her feet, her only concern for the boy who stood defenseless as the Drakka approached him. She felt her *ki* flare, pulsing in her veins like a drumbeat. Guided by intuition, she dug her fingers into the dirt and funneled the power she felt into the earth. The ground between the boy and the Drakka heaved upward, soil and stone rising to form a wall that intercepted the beast.

Kai's amazement didn't last long as the Drakka roared and pummeled the earthen barrier. It held, but Kai wasn't sure how long it would remain. She could feel her strength quickly fading and suspected the barrier was powered by her *ki*. With its attention diverted, the Drakka didn't see Kai until it was too late. She plunged her blade into its back, jerked it sharply, then yanked it free.

The Drakka let out a guttural scream that echoed throughout the village, its eyes widening in disbelief as it staggered briefly and fell to its knees. Blood spurted from the wound, and the creature fell face-first onto the ground, dead. Kai gasped as a sharp pain lanced through her ribcage, and the earthen barrier crumbled.

"To the river, hurry," Kai urged the boy. He nodded, wide-eyed, and ran off. The world around Kai spun and she dropped her sword.

I don't feel so good.

The last thing she saw was the ground coming up to meet her.

CHAPTER 5

When Kai opened her eyes, she found herself in an unfamiliar place. She struggled to make sense of the scattered images that flashed through her mind, and Hikari's own barrage of memories only added to her disorientation.

What happened?

You lost consciousness, Hikari replied.

Kai propped herself up on her elbows. She was lying on a straw mat in a large open hut. Several injured people were lying on similar bedrolls, and the room was filled with hushed groans and whispered prayers. The smell of blood and smoke was thick in the air, and the iron tang stung Kai's nostrils.

Where am I?

We're still in the village. After you collapsed, a group of warriors arrived and drove the Drakka away.

Are they still here? Kai asked.

Yes. They put out the fires and are helping to salvage what remains.

Kai forced herself onto her feet and stepped out of the hut. Her senses sharpened as she took in the chaos of what remained of the village. Homes were reduced to rubble and the earth was scorched, yet despite that, Kai could sense the resilience of the villagers. Some of them were already at work clearing the debris.

A group of individuals stood near Hikari, and Kai could tell by their bearing they were the warriors the dragon spoke of. Kai approached, and one of them turned to face her.

"You're awake. I feared the Drakka's fury had claimed you."

His voice, though soft, cut through the air with a clarity that commanded attention. His gaze locked onto hers, piercing in its appraisal.

"My name is Ryn. This is your dragon?"

"Yes," Kai answered.

"She is unique. I've never seen one quite like her before. What's your name?"

"Kai."

"You don't talk much, do you?"

"Only when it's necessary. Thank you for helping me. My dragon is still learning, and I don't think she would have known what to do for me."

Ryn's brows scrunched, but he said nothing.

"What brought you here?" Kai asked. "Your timing couldn't have been better."

"We've been tracking this group of Drakka for days. I wanted to catch them before they came across any settlements, but..." he glanced around at the village and sighed. "We weren't quick enough."

"I am sure the people here appreciate your efforts regardless. You said you were tracking the Drakka... where are your dragons?"

A pained expression briefly creased the man's face. "Our dragons are no longer with us."

Kai had heard of the Sundered before. They were Sworn whose dragons had died, usually at the hands of the Drakka. Instead of returning to a normal life, they devoted themselves to fighting the creatures on their own. She offered a silent nod of understanding. While she had only been bonded to Hikari for a short time, she knew that to lose that connection was to lose a part of oneself.

"How were you able to track the beasts? They hide their movements with magic."

"Ever since I was young, I've been able to sense the Drakka's stirrings. I thought it was something I gained through my bond, but the ability remains even though my dragon is no more."

"It seems like the emperor would put that to good use," Kai said.

"He probably would if I allowed him to. When my dragon died, I severed all ties to the empire. My brethren and I forge our own path."

Kai admired his resolve, though she wondered why he didn't see the value of using his talent alongside the Sworn.

"Where is the rest of your contingent?"

Kai debated on how to answer him, and before she could speak, he said, "You are welcome to join us. You are not Sundered like us, but we're on a quest and could use your help, and that of your dragon."

"I have my own duties to attend to," she replied. "But I am curious. Why would you need our help?"

"We have a way to deal a powerful blow to the Drakka, but we are not equipped to do it on our own. That is where you and your dragon would help."

Kai wished Kokoro was with them. She trusted the elder dragon's guidance, but she knew, too, that she would not always be able to rely on her. "What is your plan?"

"The Drakka employ underground caves to hide their eggs. I have found the entrance to one. If we can get inside, we can destroy the nest."

Kai's eyes widened in surprise. The idea of destroying a Drakka nest filled her with both trepidation and excitement. Being underground to retrieve the Heart of Flame was harrowing enough, but traveling into the earth and being surrounded by Drakka was another matter entirely. It wasn't ideal, but it was a worthwhile cause if it was successful.

"Why do you need my help? You seem to have enough men for such a task."

Ryn smiled at her. "Nothing can destroy Drakka eggs except dragon fire. You should know this."

Is that true? Kai asked Hikari.

It feels true. Although they are corrupted, they are a form of dragon.

"Why not go to the Sworn? They would relish the chance to strike at the Drakka."

"I told you already. I do not align with the empire." There was something in his tone that gave Kai the impression there was more to his story than the loss of his dragon, but if he had grievances with the empire, that was his concern.

How do you feel about this? I think we should consult with Kokoro.

Hikari regarded her intently, and Kai could see her reflection in the dragon's blue eyes. *I will follow your lead in this matter. If you want Kokoro's blessing, then we shall get it... but if you want to make your own decision...*

Kai didn't need to hear Hikari finish her sentence to know the dragon would follow her regardless of the outcome.

"What assurances do we have that this will work?"

"Assurances?" Ryn scoffed. "There are no assurances in war, but with my ability, we will be one step ahead of the Drakka if they sense our presence."

Kai considered the risks. "The bond we share with our dragons is..." she paused, searching for the right words. "Deeply woven.

To have those threads torn from you... it is a wrong that cries out to be righted." She looked at Hikari, who lowered her head approvingly.

"We will help you."

CHAPTER 6

As Kai stared into the black abyss, she questioned whether she had made the right decision. Hikari walked behind her, which offered some comfort, but the idea of being trapped belowground with Drakka made her heart quicken.

It had surprised her to learn the entrance to the nest was only a few hours march from the village, but in retrospect, she suspected that was probably where the attackers had originated from.

The tunnel was wide, and the air was cool. If Kai didn't know any better, she would have no idea the tunnel led to a nest of Drakka eggs. There were no foul smells lingering in the air, and the silence was broken only by the echoes of their footsteps. Ryn and his men were ahead of her leading the way, weapons drawn and ready, while their torches cast flickering shadows that danced along the rough-hewn walls.

The further they progressed, the more Kai felt as though someone was watching her. It reminded her of the day before the storm hit Ikje.

Ikje.

She prayed that her parents were safe, and that Master Satoshi had successfully repelled the Drakka attack. The more she thought about her parents, the more homesick she grew.

I would like to meet your parents, Hikari said.

Reading my mind again?

Guilt from the dragon washed over her.

It's all right, Kai soothed. *It is odd sharing my thoughts with another, but it's also nice to have someone to share them with. I never...*

Memories of her childhood came unbidden, flowing through the bond. She was alone.

There was no one to talk with, and other children were forbidden from playing with her. The emptiness she felt stung her even now, and her eyes welled with tears. She blinked them away.

You are not alone any longer.

Hikari's words comforted her like nothing else.

Thank you for bonding with me, Kai said.

Thank you for awakening me. I don't know how long I slept, but it was far too long.

As they continued their trek, Kai's thoughts turned back to the task at hand. The air grew heavy and warm, and a faint odor began to permeate the darkness. Ryn held up a hand, bringing everyone to a halt. He crouched down, briefly examining the ground, then rose back up and motioned for everyone to continue.

The tunnel branched in two different directions, and Ryn led them along the path to the right. After roughly fifty feet, the tunnel opened into an enormous chamber. Along the top of the cavern, moss gave off an eerie fluorescent green glow, illuminating hundreds of dark eggs that lay nestled in earthen cradles. Kai froze as she took in the sight.

"There are so many," she said.

"And this is only one of their nests," Ryn replied. "Once your dragon burns the shells, we need to drive our swords into what remains to ensure they are truly dead."

Kai nodded and looked at Hikari. The dragon rumbled, the sound echoing in the vast, hollow chamber that acted as a womb within the earth. She trudged forward and leaned her head down, expelling a torrent of flames on the nearest eggs. The heat washed over Kai, and she had to take a few steps back from the intensity. The fire faded, and the eggs smoldered, small tendrils of smoke rising into the air.

Ryn and his men set about driving their blades into the shells. Kai watched them as they worked. These were hardened men. There was no hesitation in their strikes, no mercy. As the Sundered moved from one mound to another, their armor whispered with their movements. Feeling useless, Kai walked over to inspect their work.

The shells were as dark as her sword, though it was hard for her to determine if that was their natural color or from Hikari's flames. The punctures from the swords oozed inky liquid, and in one of them, she saw the small face of a Drakka, its mouth opened in a silent cry.

Guilt washed over her, and she turned away from the gruesome sight. She knew what was at stake, understood what needed to be done, but to destroy life before it had a chance to begin was a grim task. She took a deep breath and steeled herself, then drew her sword and joined the Sundered.

Kai's fingers tightened around the hilt of her ebony blade in a steadfast grip. With deliberate steps, she advanced to the nearest clutch of eggs and paused. The moment stretched taut as she raised the blade, the metal catching the light of the moss above in a sinister gleam. Her resolve faltered, and her hand tremored.

We do what we must, Hikari told her. *We are the shield against the darkness, the sword against chaos. We are not killing innocent creatures.*

Emboldened by her dragon's words, she thrusted the sword forward. The impact of steel upon shell sent a resonant clang throughout the chamber, the sound magnified by the hollowness of the cave. Kai plunged her sword into another egg. Shards flew. One after another, the eggs fell to her black blade.

The air grew fouler as they worked. The ichor that leaked from the eggs smelled like dead animals, and Kai's nostrils flared as she stifled a cough. She forced herself to breathe through her mouth, but she didn't find it much better since she felt as though she could taste the stench.

"Hold!" Ryn shouted.

All sounds ceased, and Kai glanced at him to see why they had stopped. After a tense moment that seemed to last an eternity, he said, "Continue."

The metallic chorus resumed, and after several minutes, Kai paused to wipe the sweat from her brow. Her arms ached from the effort, and judging by how much of the cavern they hadn't covered yet, she estimated they weren't even halfway done yet.

"This is taking too long," she said aloud.

"Press on," Ryn urged. "We don't have much time."

"Are the Drakka coming?"

His lack of an answer was all she needed. Kai glanced around the chamber, looking for an exit, but the light of the moss only illuminated so much, and everything else remained hidden in the shadows.

Do you see another way out of here? she asked Hikari.

There was a pause, and the dragon replied. *There is not.*

"We need to leave while we can," she told Ryn. "If the Drakka corner us in here..."

Ryn yanked his sword from an egg and turned to her, a wild look in his eyes. He was consumed with bloodlust.

"If we die, then we die with honor," he snarled.

The other Sundered stopped and looked at him. Kai could tell they weren't all in agreement with his words.

"Your grief is my grief," one of the men said. "But hope has not fled from us. If the Drakka are drawing close, I want to fight them on our terms, not theirs. Kai is right. If they catch us in here, we will all die."

Ryn's intensity diminished, and when he spoke, his words were calmer. "I-I'm sorry. You are both right. I let my hatred for these creatures get the better of me. We have done what we can for now. Let us leave, and we can return to finish this later."

Kai was glad he could be reasoned with. She didn't want to leave the Sundered down here, but she also wasn't going to risk death to destroy a few more eggs. Ryn sheathed his blade and marched across the cavern, heading back the way they'd entered.

"Wait," one of the Sundered said. "There's something there, in the darkness."

"What is it?" Ryn asked.

"I'm not sure. You should look at it."

Ryn hesitated, but he turned around and walked over to where the man stood. He knelt and inspected where the man indicated.

"There's nothing—"

The man struck Ryn in the side of the head, knocking him to the ground.

"Have you lost your mind, Shuji? What are you doing?"

The man, Shuji, pressed the tip of his sword to Ryn's throat.

"No one is going anywhere until Kai gives me her dragon."

CHAPTER 7

"Shuji, you fool! You can't bond with the dragon. She's already bound to Kai."

"I'm not the one that wants her," Shuji replied. "The Drakka do."

Kai stared in disbelief at him. She barely knew these men, but she would never have suspected any of them would side with their enemy.

"You would betray your oath?" Ryn spat.

"My oath died with my dragon." Shuji paused, glancing at the other Sundered before his gaze fell on Kai. "I'm sorry," he said. "The Drakka have power beyond imagining. Our fight is a lost cause, and I would rather live under their rule than die. Make your choice now."

"Or what?" Kai asked.

"Or I'll kill Ryn. His blood will be on your hands."

"If you kill him, you won't get far before Hikari flames you to death."

"I'll take my chances," Shuji said, pressing his sword down and nicking Ryn's neck. A trickle of blood ran down his flesh.

Kai's hand trembled on the hilt of her sword, her mind racing through the impossible decision before her. The tension among the other Sundered was almost palpable.

"Your life will not be worth living under the Drakka," Kai said. "They consume everything. You know this. They may let you live for a time, but they will eventually consume you as well."

"I have no choice. They have my family."

"We will help you free them," Ryn said.

For a moment, Kai thought Shuji would be swayed, but her hopes were dashed when he shook his head.

"Your words feel like silk, but they are nothing more than cobwebs in the wind. Now, choose."

Hikari sniffed the air, turning her head toward the tunnel. *They are coming.*

"Time is running out," Shuji taunted.

Kai took a step toward the traitor, and he pressed his blade deeper into Ryn's neck, forcing her to stop. "Let him go," she pleaded.

"Give me your dragon and I will."

"That will never happen."

"Then you will all die here and the Drakka will take her anyway."

As if his words had summoned them, Drakka began to pour into the chamber from the tunnel. Kai's eyes widened in fear, but it was quickly driven away by anger. It sparked within her, swelling into a roaring inferno. With a defiant cry, she tapped into the bond, pulling from a hidden wellspring of power. It surged forth like a tidal wave, a torrent of energy that filled her very veins, setting every fiber of her being ablaze.

Her sword reacted to the power; its edge hungry for the blood of the Drakka. It came alight with an ethereal glow, and Kai drove the blade into the ground. The air itself seemed to scream, charged with the raw energy that poured from her. It was as if the souls of the elders lent their strength to her, guiding her hand. An aura of black light enveloped her, and the chamber quaked. The Drakka halted, looking around in confusion.

"Let him go," Kai demanded, her voice echoing through the cavern.

Shuji's eyes darted between her and the Drakka. Kai could sense his internal battle, torn between his loyalty to Ryn and his desire to see his family safe. Finally, he lifted his sword from Ryn's throat, his eyes never leaving Kai's. The other Sundered seized his sword and pushed him toward the Drakka.

The creatures charged, their confusion replaced with fury. Shuji was cut down mercilessly, and Kai felt a pang of sadness at his death. He had fallen for their tricks and betrayed his own kind. That thought fueled her anger further, and she rushed forward to meet the Drakka, her sword slicing through the air. She severed the heads of those closest, and Hikari joined her, blasting a stream of flames into the Drakka's ranks.

Their screams echoed in the cave as they fell, but their fellows weren't swayed. They continued to stream in from the tunnel, their numbers unending. Emboldened by her display, Ryn and the other Sundered fell in beside her, hacking and slashing.

Despite their valiant stand, Kai knew the power coursing through her wouldn't last forever. She scanned the chamber, looking for a way out, or at least some way to stall for time. And then she saw it, a hidden passage half concealed by a rockslide.

"There," she shouted, pointing with her sword. "Move that way!"

The Sundered followed her direction, slowly turning their back to it and retreating.

Can you move those rocks? Kai asked Hikari.

I will not leave your side.

You must. It's our only way to escape.

The dragon snarled and released another wave of flames, then bounded away. Kai thrusted her sword into a Drakka and began walking backwards alongside the Sundered. With Hikari gone, the Drakka crowded in closer, threatening to encircle them. A rumble filled the chamber as the stones were moved, and then Hikari was at Kai's side again, swatting Drakka aside with her claws.

The way is clear.

"Everyone into the tunnel! Hikari and I will hold them off!"

The Sundered broke away and ran for the exit. Kai could feel the power she had tapped into rapidly dwindling. Once the men were safe, Kai urged her dragon to go next.

You first, Hikari said.

I have a plan, and I don't want you in the way of what's coming.

Hikari's concern was evident in the bond, but she relented and hurried into the tunnel. Kai turned and sprinted for the opening, sliding to a halt as she reached the threshold. She turned back to face the Drakka and drew in a deep breath, hoping that whatever was guiding her wasn't leading her astray.

She held her black blade out before her and closed her eyes, pooling the remaining energy into the obsidian stone in the pommel. The sounds of the approaching Drakka faded, and time seemed to stand still. Warmth radiated from the stone, growing hotter with each passing moment. Kai could feel the energy preparing to burst forth, and her skin prickled with anticipation.

A flash of light blinded Kai even though her eyes were closed, and she was thrown backwards as the last of her energy was released in a violent burst. As the light faded, she lay gasping in the tunnel, her strength gone. After a few moments, she sat up, but her vision swam, and she slumped against the wall. When the nausea passed, she looked into the cavern.

Tendrils of smoke rose from the stone floor. The Drakka were gone, their bodies reduced to ash. Kai took a shaky breath and rose to her feet. Her legs felt as though they were made of jelly, but they held her up. She had no idea how she had wielded such power, but it had saved them. The cost was great, and she didn't know if you would be able to do it again. She searched for the well of power, but it was gone, no trace of it remained.

Kai was startled from her reverie when she heard footsteps, but it was only Ryn. He stared at her like she was a strange creature he'd just stumbled upon, but he offered her his hand. She accepted it and he helped her up the tunnel.

How did I do that? she asked Hikari.

I could feel the elders of the past guiding you, but otherwise, I do not know. Perhaps Kokoro will have the answer.

They navigated their way through the passageway in silence, eventually stepping out into daylight. Kai sat on the ground and noticed the Sundered were staring at her.

"What is it?"

"You are the Blooded One," Ryn said. As one, they all lowered to their knees and bowed to her.

"What are you doing? Get up."

"We are swearing fealty to you, Kai. You are the one spoken of in the scrolls, and we will follow you against the Drakka."

CHAPTER 8

Despite Kai's protests, the Sundered insisted on following her and Hikari to Tatenagawa. They shared a meal to replenish their strength, and after a brief rest, Kai stood and walked over to the dragon, running a hand along her scales.

"We shouldn't stay here long," Ryn said, coming over to join Kai. "The Drakka are regrouping. You and your dragon should go. We'll meet you at the temple."

"On foot? If the Drakka catch you—"

"They won't," Ryn promised. "We know this land better than those creatures ever will." He clasped her on the shoulder, his grip firm but not unkind. "What you did down there… I've never seen anything like it. I know you will turn the tides of this war."

Kai doubted that was true, but she didn't say it. If the man believed it, who was she to tell him otherwise?

"I will see you at Tatenagawa, then," she said.

Hikari crouched low, and Kai climbed onto her back. She offered a nod to Ryn, who bowed his head respectfully.

I'm ready, she told Hikari.

The dragon spread her wings and took off, climbing into the sky. Kai watched the Sundered grow smaller, then turned her gaze ahead. It was an odd feeling having others view her as some sort of savior. She had never sought attention or fame, nor did she want it now, but if Kokoro was right, then Kai *was* the one from the prophecy…

The wind whipped at Kai's hair, and she turned her thoughts to her parents. She missed them dearly. How did they feel that their other daughter had sided with the

Drakka? Were they appalled? Did they blame themselves for the path her life had taken?

Kai envisioned her sister, which wasn't difficult. They were twins, and their features were so similar that when Kai had seen her, she thought she was seeing an apparition.

As the temple's sloped roof came into view, she could see smoke rising into the air.

Do you see that? Kai asked.

Yes.

Hikari picked up speed, cutting through the air so quickly that Kai could feel her grip on the dragon's scales loosening. The temple grounds were overrun when they landed. Hikari set down in the courtyard, and Kai leaped down from her back and drew her sword.

A dozen Drakka were trying to break through the temple doors, but Hikari dispatched them with a blaze of fire. Kai kicked their charred remains aside and pounded on the door.

"Kokoro! Are you all right?"

There was only silence, and Kai's heart raced as she considered the worst. The doors swung open, and Kokoro stepped out to meet her.

"You arrived just in time," the elder said. "With your help, we can drive them away."

"Have they attacked the temple before?"

"Never. They have become bold indeed if they think they will overrun these sacred grounds."

"Where is Liu?" Kai asked.

"Here," he answered, exiting the temple. He was wearing his armor and had his sword in his right hand.

"He wouldn't leave my side," Kokoro said. "As if I need a protector. Come, let us make these Drakka regret ever stepping foot here."

The three of them spread out in front of Hikari. Kai stood to Kokoro's left, and Liu stood to the elder's right. A group of Drakka came around the side of the temple and shouted battle cries, rushing toward them.

Kai and Liu charged ahead to meet them while Kokoro stayed close to Hikari. They were outnumbered by the Drakka, but they had the advantage of Hikari's flames. Liu and Kai met them head-on, their swords clashing against the Drakka's weapons.

Kai ducked under a sweeping blow, then thrust her black blade into the creature's midsection. The Drakka let out a roar before collapsing to the ground. She pulled her sword free and finished it off, then turned to the next attacker. She tried to parry a strike, but she was no match for the creature's brute strength, and she staggered back from the blow.

Liu came to her aid, his blade separating both of the Drakka's arms at the elbow. Dark blood spurted onto the cobblestones, and Liu swung his sword in an arc, removing its head. Its body toppled to the ground.

"Thank you," Kai said breathlessly. Liu nodded in reply, engaging another of the Drakka.

The two continued to cut through the Drakka's ranks, but Kai could feel her strength waning. It had been a long day, and exhaustion was setting in. She took a moment to glance at Kokoro.

"Use the heart," the elder urged.

"What do you mean?"

Kokoro's words were drowned out by the clash of steel, and Kai turned her attention back to the Drakka in time to see a clawed hand. It struck her in the head, and the next thing she knew, she was lying on the ground staring up at the sky.

She groaned as she sat up and forced herself back onto her feet. Liu was surrounded, and Kai cursed under her breath. She grabbed her sword off the ground and rushed forward, driving it into the back of the nearest Drakka. Wrenching the blade free, she thrusted the tip of the blade into the neck of another.

Get down, Hikari warned Kai.

She looked at the dragon and could see the dragon's throat glowing with orange light.

"Down!" she shouted, tackling Liu to the ground. An intense heat washed over her as

Hikari flamed the Drakka. Kai rolled around, fearing her clothes had caught fire, but she was unscathed. Hikari's precision was miraculous.

Impressive.

Thank you, Hikari replied, her pride filling the bond.

Kai helped Liu back up, then brushed ash from her clothes.

"That was a small force," Kokoro said. "I fear more will come. It is obvious to me that your sister is directing them."

Liu sheathed his blade. "Let them come. We will slay them all."

"Do not speak foolishly," Kokoro chastised him. "We are outnumbered, and there are no allies nearby."

"While Hikari and I were gone, we met a group of Sundered. They have pledged to help us against the Drakka. They are on their way here."

"How many do they number?"

"Only a handful, but they are skilled warriors."

"It is not enough," Kokoro said.

"You can transform into your true self. I am sure the Drakka would cower and flee at the sight."

Kokoro smiled sadly. "I suppose they would, but it is not possible. My spirit fades, and with it, my power. I hope to complete your training before..."

Kai frowned. "Before what? Do you mean you are dying?"

"Yes, I am dying. I have lived longer than any of my kind before me, and I am weary."

"But we need you," Kai said. "We cannot defeat the Drakka without you."

"You will be fine without me. I sensed a great power while you were gone. It was you, wasn't it?"

Kai nodded.

"Tell me what happened."

CHAPTER 9

The setting sun cast long shadows across the courtyard as Kai recounted the events from her quest at the volcano. Kokoro listened intently, and her expression was grave as Kai finished.

"You showed great courage entering the nest of the Drakka, but your greatest trial lies ahead."

"What do you mean?" Kai asked.

"To defeat the Drakka is one thing, but to face your own kind is another. Can you strike down your own flesh and blood? Your sister?"

The question left Kai speechless. She stared at the elder in silence, her thoughts racing from one scenario to another.

"I cannot answer that. Not now, at least. It's not something I'd considered. I was hoping…"

"That you could save her somehow?" Kokoro smiled sadly. "It is a pleasant thought, but I do not see any hope for that. In the end, it will be you or her. Only one can prevail."

"It can't be that simple," Kai argued. "I know I don't know her, but it doesn't feel right."

"It is not simple," Kokoro replied. "But it is necessary. You should prepare yourself for what must be done. But enough of that. There is another matter we must discuss."

Kai was thankful for the change of subject. The thought of fighting her sister, let alone killing her, was hard to imagine. And yet, she knew what was at stake was much greater than any sibling loyalty. The fate of the empire hung in the balance.

"There is another item that will help you to defeat the Drakka. It has long been hidden from human eyes."

"What is it?" Kai asked.

"I had hoped to never speak of this relic, let alone see it used again. But desperate times call for desperate measures."

As Kokoro explained the nature of the item, Kai listened with a mixture of fear and awe. A cloak made from the hide of an elder dragon? The ability to move between what was visible and invisible? It seemed unbelievable, yet Kokoro had also told her of the Heart of Flame, and that was real.

"The shadow realm," Kai repeated, murmuring the words.

"It is a place where light and dark coexist, and time flows differently. It is a realm of great power and even greater danger. The cloak allows its wearer to traverse the boundaries between our world and the shadow realm, granting them abilities beyond mortal sight."

Kai ran her fingers along her leg. She found a seam and ran it under her nails. "If this artifact is so powerful, why has it been hidden away? Why has it not been used before?"

"Power always comes with a price. The cloak is as much a burden as it is a blessing. It has driven many to madness, consuming them with the allure of its abilities."

Kai's unease caused her voice to break when she asked, "And you think I can wield it without succumbing to its influence?"

"Your heart is pure, and your intentions noble... but make no mistake, using it will test you in ways you cannot yet imagine. With your dragon's strength behind you, I am confident you will not be swayed."

"I will do what is needed."

"Very good," Kokoro said. "Rest while you can. You will need to leave in the morning."

The elder took her leave, returning to the temple. Kai was tired, but there was too much on her mind. She found a bamboo bucket and began cleaning the remains of the Drakka from the courtyard. Considering they were piles of ash, it didn't take long for her to cleanse the grounds of the creatures. She washed the bucket out in the river, then filled it with water and scrubbed the cobblestones by hand. Kai could feel Liu's gaze on her as she worked.

"You have grown much in a short time," he said.

"It doesn't feel like it."

"That is because you are focused on where you are going, and not where you are or where you've been. When you only think about the future, you lose sight of the past."

Kai had to admit there was truth to his words, but she didn't say anything.

"You've become stronger, wiser, and more determined." He paused. "But there is one thing that I haven't seen change in you. Your compassion. It's what makes you different from other riders."

"It's not my intention to be different," Kai said, ceasing her scrubbing for a moment and looking up at him.

"Of course not. That's not what I was implying. I merely mean that you don't see the world the same as others. That's not a bad thing."

Kai smiled slightly, then continued her task. "Do you think Kokoro is right about me? That I can use the cloak?"

"That remains to be seen, but I believe in you."

Kai's cheeks flushed. When she'd first met him, she thought he was nothing more than a rough soldier who'd been assigned as her guard. The more she got to know him, the more she realized there was more to him than a sword and armor. He was her friend.

"Thank you," she said softly.

"For what?"

"Everything."

"I haven't done much besides teach you to wield a blade," he said, chuckling. "But you're welcome."

Once Kai felt the courtyard was properly cleaned, she returned to the river and washed the sweat and grime from herself. The cool water soothed her aching muscles, and she felt somewhat rejuvenated. Hikari laid on the grass nearby, and Kai felt vulnerable enough to remove her clothes and clean them. By the time she set them on the riverbank to dry, the sun was gone. Hikari used her breath to warm them, and after a few moments, the moisture had vanished.

Kai dried herself as best as she could, then put her clothes back on and laid on the grass beside Hikari, watching the stars twinkle into existence. She closed her eyes, feeling the weight of the day on her mind and body.

As she slept, she dreamed of battling the Drakka, of mastering the power of the cloak, and of facing her sister. When she awoke, the sun was beginning to rise. Kai sat up, startled she'd slept so long.

"Ah," she groaned, rubbing her stiff neck muscles. "Why did you let me fall asleep out here?"

I didn't want to disturb your rest, Hikari replied. *It was also nice to have some company, even if you weren't coherent.*

Kai got to her feet and stretched, then rubbed the sleep from her eyes. Her stomach growled, and she realized she hadn't eaten anything before falling asleep. She made her way to the temple and found Liu standing in the courtyard eating rice cakes. He offered her some, and she devoured several of them eagerly.

"You're not hungry, are you?" A smile tugged at his lips.

"I've never felt hungrier," Kai said, taking another rice cake from his plate and biting into it. "I don't think I moved the entire night."

"Using magic has that effect," Kokoro said as she joined them. "You must be careful not to push yourself too hard."

Kai finished chewing and wiped her mouth with the back of her hand. "Where is this cloak I need to find?"

Kokoro pointed north. "A crypt lies in Shaoing beyond the Shinraha Mountains. Spectral guardians protect it and will challenge you."

"What kind of challenges will they pose?"

"Tests of will, wisdom, and courage. You must pass them all to obtain the cloak. Liu, I want you to go with her. Hikari should be able to carry you both, and Kai will need your help."

Liu bowed his head respectfully.

"I have packed you some supplies for the journey. It will take you at least two days, for Hikari will not be able to fly the entire way without rest. Be wary. Shaoing was once protected by my brother, but he has been gone many years, and I am sure the Drakka have taken over his temple."

"We will be careful," Liu said, taking the pack of supplies from Kokoro. "And we will return as quickly as possible."

Kai was grateful for his confidence. The only thing running through her mind was one question.

Am I truly ready for this?

CHAPTER 10

The sun cast a golden hue over the jagged peaks of the Shinraha Mountains. Their snow-capped summits gleamed, and a chill wind nipped at Kai's flesh. She kept her eyes on the horizon, the monotony of the landscape below broken by the occasional glimpse of wild game.

Liu was seated behind her, his hands resting on her waist. Under normal circumstances, it would have made her feel uncomfortable, but she knew he was merely holding onto her to keep from being pulled away by the wind. There was nothing more to his loose embrace, and she appreciated the warmth that radiated from him.

They had been flying for a few hours, and Kai could sense the fatigue in Hikari's wing beats. She patted the dragon on the neck comfortingly.

You should rest, she said.

Hikari snorted in response, sending tendrils of smoke into the air that quickly dissipated.

Land at the next clearing, Kai insisted.

A few moments later, Hikari descended to the base of the mountains. They landed with a soft thud, and Kai slid down the dragon's shoulder, her legs aching from the hours of riding. The wind howled between the peaks, the sound almost like distant voices.

"I'll build a fire," Liu offered.

As he set about collecting wood, Kai wrapped her arms around herself. The air was cold and thin, and it bit into her bones even through her clothes. She hoped Hikari wouldn't need long to rest. She hated the cold.

Liu placed several sticks in a pile and drew his sword, swiftly sliding a stone up and down the edge of the blade. A few sparks came to life, but it wasn't enough to ignite the wood.

"Watch out," Kai said.

Liu looked up just as Hikari huffed, expelling a small ball of flame that struck the pile and set the wood alight. He sheathed his sword and sat down, holding his hands out near the fire. Kai sat down opposite him and huddled as close to the flames as she dared. Hikari curled into a ball behind her and was soon asleep.

Kai watched the flames dance, lost in her thoughts. She thought of her sister again and wondered how life would have been had things gone differently. Would they have still shared a bond with the same dragon? Or would one of them have faded from the bond for the benefit of the other?

Perhaps it wouldn't have been her sitting here in the cold mountains on a quest to find an ancient crypt, but Akuhara instead. Kai looked up from the fire to see Liu staring at her.

He broke the silence, his voice soft but edged with curiosity. "Are you all right? You look upset."

"I'm just thinking."

"You're thinking about *her,* aren't you? Your sister?"

"Yes. It feels wrong to abandon any hope of saving her, but you heard Kokoro. She thinks there is no salvation for her."

"Things don't always unfold the way we wish they did," Liu said. "I know that doesn't help nor comfort you, but life is harsh. We must weather these things as best as we can without losing our humanity."

Hikari stirred in her sleep, and Kai glanced at her.

"Do you think dragons feel things like we do?"

Liu's brow furrowed as he considered the question. "I think they feel everything more deeply than we know. But they don't dwell on the past like we do. They live in the now, in the heart of the moment. Maybe that's something we can learn from them."

Kai contemplated his words. Maybe he was right. She couldn't control the events of the past, but she could sway events happening now. The wind howled again, louder this time, and Kai's gaze traveled to a rocky ridge. The sound was different—less like the wind and more like something alive.

Liu noticed it, too. His hand drifted to the hilt of his sword. "Did you hear that?"

Kai stood, her muscles tensing as she peered beyond Hikari's bulk. Her breath hitched when she saw them—hulking forms, their silhouettes unmistakable. They were trudging down from the mountains.

"Drakka," Kai hissed. "Put out the fire!"

Liu was already a step ahead of her, shoveling dirt with his hands and dumping it onto the flames.

"How many?" he asked.

"Too many."

"Have they seen us?"

Kai hesitated. "I don't think so."

They waited in silence and watched as the Drakka passed by their location. The creatures moved in a slow, methodical line, far different from their usual behavior. Kai counted at least twenty, their bodies rippling with unnatural strength.

When the last of them disappeared from view, Kai let out a sigh. "We got lucky. If they had seen us..."

Hikari lifted her head, sniffing at the air. *I smell Drakka nearby.*

They've passed through here already, Kai replied.

"Did you notice the direction they're heading in?" Liu asked.

Kai followed the path the Drakka took and realized they were traveling southwest. "Do you think they are going to Tatenagawa?"

He shrugged. "That's impossible to know, but Kokoro can take care of herself. We need to keep moving. If they catch our trail, we aren't in the best position to defend ourselves." Liu looked at Hikari. "Are you rested enough to continue?"

Hikari stretched her wings and yawned. Kai could feel the dragon's weariness had lessened, but her strength wasn't fully restored.

I can manage, Hikari said, projecting her thoughts for both of them to hear.

Are you sure? Kai asked.

Yes.

The sun was in the middle of the sky, but despite it being midday, the temperature seemed to be getting colder. Kai wanted to give Hikari more time to rest, but she also wanted to be gone from this place.

Let us get moving, then. We will stop again at nightfall unless you can't make it that far. There is no need to push yourself beyond your limits.

Hikari rumbled her agreement, and Kai and Liu climbed onto her back. The wind picked up as they took to the air, but Kai ignored the chill. They soared above the snowy peaks, and the air grew so cold Kai could see her breath puff out in small clouds.

They flew until they were beyond the bulk of the mountains. The air grew gradually warmer, and Kai pointed to a grove of trees.

We'll camp there for the night, Kai said. *It'll provide cover and we should be able to keep a fire going without worrying about prying eyes.*

Hikari took them down, landing just outside of the tree line. Liu and Kai went to work setting up camp while Hikari went hunting for food. They soon had a crackling fire going, and they shared a meal of fresh fruit and fish from the supplies Kokoro had given them.

The wind eased as night engulfed the land, and the stars shined above the tree canopy. Kai's belly was full, and she lounged beside the fire, her eyes heavy. She was surprised how tiring it was doing much of nothing.

"I'll take first watch while you get some sleep," Liu offered.

Kai laid her head down on her arms and closed her eyes, drifting off to sleep. Once again, strange dreams haunted her.

CHAPTER 11

Kai awoke to the chirping of birds. She blinked several times, confused at where she was. Slowly, her wits returned, and she stared at the charred wood and ash, all that remained of the fire from the night before.

She sat up and looked around, rubbing her eyes. Liu was asleep, but Hikari was awake, keeping a vigilant eye over them.

Did you find food? Kai asked.

I found a few deer, the dragon replied. *And I slept while Liu kept watch. He was going to wake you, but I couldn't sleep anymore, so I took over.*

Thank you. I needed that.

Kai rose to her feet and stretched. She'd slept longer than she expected, and she felt fully refreshed.

I scouted ahead last night. We aren't far from Shaoing.

How much further is it?

A few hours, Hikari replied.

Kai rummaged through the bag of food Kokoro had given them and settled on a rice cake wrapped in seaweed. She ate in silence and enjoyed the sights and sounds of the woods around her. Wandering away from the camp, she relieved herself among some bushes and found a small stream where she splashed ice-cold water on her face. She drank her fill and returned to the camp, gently shaking Liu until his eyes snapped open.

"Time to get moving," she said. "Hikari says we'll reach Shaoing today."

Liu grunted and got up, rubbing sleep from his eyes. He ate a rice cake and drank from the stream, then packed their meager belongings. They were gone soon after, cutting through the morning air on Hikari's back.

A few hours later, just as Hikari had said, Shaoing came into view. A monolithic structure of weathered stone stretched skyward, its crumbling walls marred by deep cracks and overgrown with twisted vines.

Hikari landed in front of the temple, a low growl rumbling in her chest. *This place is not natural. It has been shaped by something old… powerful.*

Kai dismounted and slid to the ground, her boots sinking into the damp earth. She could faintly sense what Hikari was talking about. There was something in the air, a humming of some kind, but when she tried to focus on where the sound was coming from, it changed direction on her.

Do you sense any Drakka? Kai asked.

Hikari sniffed the air and snorted, her nostrils flaring. *I only smell the stench of decay.*

Massive stones had collapsed over the entrance of the temple, leaving an opening too small for the dragon. As much as she didn't like the idea of leaving Hikari behind, the dragon would have to wait outside for them.

"Liu and I will go inside," she said aloud. "If something happens, I will let you know."

Hikari stepped forward and attempted to lift the stones out of the way, but they were too heavy even for her. She grumbled and retreated, admitting defeat.

We'll be back, Kai promised.

Together, she and Liu crawled on all fours through the opening and entered the darkness of the temple. Once they were past the boulders and across the threshold of the doorway, they were able to stand. Kai's eyes struggled to adjust to the gloom. Pale, phosphorescent lichen clung to the walls, casting a glow that did little to dispel the darkness.

"Stay close," Liu said, stepping in front of her. "We don't know what sort of traps might lurk in these halls."

They made their way forward slowly, and the narrow hall they were in opened into a large antechamber. The walls were bare, and the stone floor was littered with dirt and small rocks.

"This place feels like it's been abandoned for a long time," Kai whispered, her eyes darting around the room for any sign of the guardians Kokoro had warned her about.

As if summoned by her thoughts, a shadow detached from the wall. It was tall, cloaked in dark robes that blended in with the stones. The figure moved with an unnatural grace, its face hidden beneath a hood. Kai's hand tightened on the hilt of her sword, but it made no move to attack. It stopped several paces away and pulled its hood back, revealing a skeletal face marked with runes. Where its eyes should have been were golden orbs that burned with fire.

"Why do you tread here?"

Its voice caused a chill to crawl down Kai's back. She glanced at Liu, who kept his gaze on the figure, his sword partially unsheathed. Pushing her fear aside, Kai said, "I seek the cloak."

"You must prove yourself worthy," the guardian replied.

"How do I do that?"

"Face the trials. If you are worthy, you will be given the cloak. If you fail, you will die."

The guardian's last word echoed ominously off the walls. Kokoro had mentioned it would be dangerous, true, but she hadn't said anything about possibly dying. Kai swallowed hard.

"You don't have to do this," Liu said.

"I know," she replied.

Although she knew his words were true, she felt like she didn't have a choice. Kokoro hadn't steered her wrong yet, but the threat of death gave her pause. Kai thought of her parents, of the innocent people across the empire who suffered from the Drakka. If she could save even one life by risking her own, was it worth it? She thought it was.

"I accept," she said.

The guardian's orbs glowed brighter. "Very well. Hear my riddles and answer correctly to pass forth. I am not alive, but I grow; I don't have lungs, but I need air; I don't have a mouth, but water drowns me. What am I?"

Kai repeated the words within her mind. *Not alive... grows... needs air... water drowns it.* Her eyes widened with realization. "The answer is fire."

"Correct," the guardian said, a hint of approval in its ethereal features. "I am invisible, but I carry clouds; I am weightless, but I can move the strongest tree; I have no voice, but I make whispers and howls. What am I?"

"Wind," Kai answered, relieved the riddle was easy. She wondered how many of these she would need to answer.

"Correct. I am not alive, but I cradle life; I am patient, and I shape mountains with time; I wear no clothes, but flowers adorn me. What am I?"

"Any ideas?" Kai asked Liu.

"No!" the guardian hissed. "Only you may answer."

Kai considered the riddle for a moment, unsure of what could not be alive but could shape mountains. Her first guess was the wind, but that was the answer of the last question, and flowers didn't adorn the wind. She opened her mouth, then closed it, doubting herself. Finally, she decided on an answer. "The earth?"

"Correct." The guardian's skeletal face turned serious. "Here is your final riddle. I have no shape, but I can fill any form; I am silent, but I can also roar; I am gentle, but I can carve stone. What am I?"

Kai's mind was blank. She looked at Liu again, the panic on her face obvious. He couldn't give her the answer, but maybe he could provide some sort of clue.

"The other questions are all connected," Liu said. "What connects them?"

The guardian didn't object, so Kai assumed Liu's help was acceptable. She considered the other answers. Fire, wind, earth... they were all elements.

"Water," she answered.

"Correct. You have proven your wit. You may advance to the next chamber."

The guardian's form flickered briefly and then dissipated in a flash of light, scattering motes of dust.

"Thank you," Kai said. "That almost ended in disaster."

CHAPTER 12

Upon exiting the chamber, they found themselves in a hallway. Kai expected another apparition to confront them. Instead, they found the corridor was empty. Strange symbols were carved into the walls, pulsing with an eerie glow. Kai reached out, her fingers hovering inches from a particularly intricate carving. It resembled a dragon's eye, and as she watched, the pupil dilated, focusing on her. She jerked her hand back.

"Did you see that?" she asked.

"See what?"

She stared at the symbol for a moment, waiting, but nothing happened. "Never mind. Maybe I'm seeing things."

They pressed on, navigating the winding passage. The symbols seemed to guide the way, glowing brighter as they approached intersections and dimming as they passed. Kai was lost in her thoughts, and Liu startled her when he suddenly stopped and grabbed onto her arm.

"Look."

Ahead, the hall opened into a vast chamber, this one bigger than the last, and its floor was covered with stone tiles. Some bore the same glowing symbols as the walls, while others remained dark.

"This feels too easy," Liu said. "I think it might be a trap."

Kai took a cautious step forward, placing her foot on a tile bearing the familiar dragon eye symbol. It glowed brighter beneath her weight, but nothing else happened.

"I think we need to follow the path of symbols. The dark tiles probably trigger something."

Liu nodded. "That makes sense. Do you want me to go first?"

"No, I'll go."

Kai took another careful step, her body tense, ready to react at the slightest sign of danger. With each successful step, her confidence grew, but so did the pressure. One mistake could mean the difference between reaching the cloak and failing not just herself, but everyone. The glowing markings emitted heat, and the room became oppressively hot. Sweat was beading on her brow by the time she neared the exit.

She hopped from the final tile to the threshold of an archway that led to a corridor with a dirt floor. Liu followed the path she had taken, and when he reached her side, they continued ahead side by side. A few steps in, the stone walls groaned and scraped as they twisted, sliding like immense puzzle pieces to form a labyrinth.

"I saw another door back there. Maybe we can—" Liu's words were cut off by a resounding thud as a stone slab fell behind them, blocking the doorway. There was no going back.

The labyrinth walls hummed with energy, and Kai rested a hand on one to see if she was supposed to use magic to direct the maze. The stone was cold and unyielding, but there was a strange vibration beneath its surface. A soft, rhythmic pulse, almost like—

Liu stepped past her, and the ground beneath her feet trembled. Kai pulled him backward. The walls shifted again, the stones grinding together as they formed a completely different path.

Kai frowned. "It changed." The walls that had been stationary moments ago had rearranged themselves as if they were alive.

"We need to move before it closes us in or crushes us," Liu said. He started forward again, but Kai hesitated.

He was right, but something about the way the walls moved—deliberate, methodical—didn't make sense. She looked down the corridor that had just opened in front of them, then to the side where another path had formed. The stones continued to grind and shift, but Kai wasn't listening to the sound of the walls. She was focused on the space between the noise, the stillness that came before each movement. There was a pattern. She could feel it, faint and elusive, but it was there.

"This place isn't just a maze," she said slowly. "It's testing us."

"What do you mean?"

"It's not about finding the right path. It's reacting to us, to how we move. We can't just charge through it."

"If we stand here, we're dead. Let's go this way." Liu strode to the left, but another tremor shook the floor, and the corridor sealed shut with a heavy slam. Kai's mind raced. The walls weren't moving randomly. They were trying to force them to make hasty decisions. It wanted them to panic. She didn't know how she knew that, she just... knew.

"Every time we move, it changes. But if we stand still..." Kai held Liu in place and gestured to the corridor in front them. It remained open, though the walls trembled slightly. "It waits."

Liu shook his head. "So what do we do? Stand here?"

"Not exactly," Kai answered, her voice firmer now. "We need to move when it lets us, not when we want to. It's like a dance."

Liu gave her a look of disbelief. "A dance with a shifting stone labyrinth that wants to crush us? Great."

"We just need to listen."

Kai closed her eyes, focusing on the subtle rhythm beneath her feet. It was like the beat of a drum. When the next shift came, she felt it in her bones.

"Now," she whispered, opening her eyes.

She stepped forward and Liu followed without hesitation. The walls stayed still for a moment longer, but as they walked, Kai could hear the low rumble of stone shifting behind them. Her heart pounded, her senses heightened. They turned a corner, and the ground trembled again, the path behind them closing off.

"Keep going," Liu urged.

"No. Wait."

Liu froze in place. Kai closed her eyes again, feeling for the pulse. The walls shifted, but only slightly. The path ahead remained open. She moved cautiously, pausing with every tremor in the stone. The labyrinth shifted around them, but now they were in sync with it, anticipating each change before it happened. The panic that had gripped Kai moments ago eased, replaced with a growing confidence.

Finally, they turned another corner and Kai saw it: a wide archway bathed in light. "That's it," she said. Liu started forward, but Kai held him back yet again. "It's not over yet."

"The exit is right there."

"I know, but it is still testing us. It wants us to rush."

The pressure in the air seemed to build as they stood there, the walls rumbling with impatience. Kai held her ground, waiting. She could feel the pulse, fainter now, but still there.

"Walk," she said. "Slowly."

Liu fell into step beside her. They moved toward the archway, and the walls groaned, but they didn't close in. As they reached the exit, the pressure lifted, and they stepped through. The labyrinth sealed shut behind them.

Liu looked at her. "Remind me never to question your instincts."

CHAPTER 13

The archway opened into a vast, tranquil garden. The ceiling above was lost in twilight, dotted with soft stars, and the ground was a lush carpet of green grass.

Kai looked around, entranced by the beauty. A soft breeze drifted through the trees, carrying the scent of cinnamon and honey. Natural winding pathways stretched out in every direction, each one lined with flowers of a different color. Statues of robed figures stood at intervals along the paths, their expressions calm and inscrutable.

"It's peaceful here," Liu said. "Too peaceful."

Kai nodded, her muscles still tense from the labyrinth. "It looks like another maze, but I don't see any logic to this one."

As they moved deeper into the garden, the paths seemed to multiply, twisting and turning until it became impossible to tell which direction they'd come from. There was no clear indication of which path to take, and every turn seemed to lead to another set of branching trails.

Kai knelt beside one of the paths and touched the flowers. They were real, soft and fragrant. But as she stood, she realized something troubling—each path seemed more enticing than the last. One was lined with radiant golden flowers, glowing softly under the twilight sky. Another was shaded by towering trees, their leaves shimmering silver. In the distance, she could hear faint music, as though someone were playing a hauntingly familiar melody just out of sight.

"Do you hear that?" she asked.

Liu tilted his head. "Music. But... where is it coming from?"

Kai's heart skipped a beat as the melody became clearer. It wasn't just any music. It was the song her mother used to hum to her when she was a child, a melody long forgotten. She swallowed hard, her throat tightening.

"We need to be careful. This place is playing tricks on us."

Kokoro had said the trials would test her will, wisdom, and courage. What sort of test was this? Every path seemed to draw her in, each one more convincing with its temptations.

"How do we figure out which path leads to the next chamber?" Liu asked.

Kai shook her head. She considered the previous tests. The garden wasn't testing her endurance or strength. Perhaps it was testing her ability to discern, to choose wisely. But how could she make a wise decision when each path felt like the right one?

Her eyes drifted to a trail lined with glowing red flowers, their petals delicate but vibrant, almost pulsing with light. The temptation was there, tugging at her, urging her to follow it. But something about it felt… wrong.

"I don't think we're supposed to follow what we want," Kai said. "I think this garden is designed to lead us astray. The more we want something, the more dangerous it becomes."

Liu glanced down a path filled with silver leaves, his eyes narrowing in suspicion. "So we should ignore everything that looks good?"

Kai didn't answer right away. Her gaze wandered over the myriad paths, the winding trails, the intoxicating smells and sights. The music tugged at her heart, but she forced herself to listen beyond it. Somewhere in this garden, there had to be a path that was true, one that wasn't about indulgence or desire.

A statue caught her attention. It stood taller than the others, its stone face worn with age, but its expression was serene. Unlike the others, this statue didn't look like a noble figure or a wise elder. It was simple, unadorned, its eyes closed as if in contemplation.

Kai walked over to stand before it. Its base was surrounded by plain white flowers, unremarkable compared to the rest of the garden. She crouched beside it, examining the inscription carved into the stone:

The true path is the one that asks for nothing.

"I think this is the correct path," she said, standing. She looked at Liu. "The other paths are trying to distract us with what we think we want, but the one we need to follow is the one that doesn't offer us anything at all."

Liu regarded the path in silence. "This one doesn't have a glow, music, or anything. If what you say is true, then you're probably right."

Kai smiled, and without waiting for his response, she stepped onto the path lined with white flowers. The moment her foot touched the trail, the distant music stopped, and the shimmering allure of the other paths seemed to dim, as though the garden itself were retreating. Liu followed, his hand on the hilt of his sword, though there was no sense of immediate danger. The path twisted and turned, but the farther they walked, the quieter it became—no illusions, no temptations.

After what felt like ages, the white flowers thinned, and the path opened into a small clearing. At the center of the clearing stood an archway similar to the one they'd passed through before, but this one was overgrown with vines.

As they approached the archway, a soft voice whispered through the garden, barely audible but familiar. It was the same voice that had sung her mother's song earlier, but this time, it held no power over her. She glanced back at the winding paths they had left behind, the colors and lights fading into the twilight as they moved closer to the exit.

Kai stopped before the archway, her mind clearer now. She understood the garden's purpose—it had shown her that wisdom wasn't always about choosing the most obvious path or the one that promised the most reward. Sometimes, the best path was the one that offered nothing in return. It was a simple lesson, but it was a heavy truth.

The vines parted to reveal a dark passageway. Kai motioned to it and looked at Liu, smiling.

"I'll let you lead this time if you want."

Liu took a long look at her before responding. "Kokoro was right to send you here. You have a connection to the magic of this place. I will follow *your* lead."

Kai laughed and gazed ahead into the darkness. She couldn't shake the feeling that something dangerous lurked within, but she had successfully navigated through all the previous challenges. Surely this one couldn't be any worse than what they had faced so far... could it?

She stepped through the archway, and Liu followed her.

CHAPTER 14

As Kai's eyes adjusted to the gloom, she saw they were in a circular chamber. The air hummed with an otherworldly energy that made the hairs on her arms stand on end. Before she could fully take in her surroundings, ethereal figures like the one from the first chamber materialized.

"We're surrounded," she whispered, grabbing the hilt of her sword. She doubted the weapon would do any good against the spirits, but the feel of it gave her a small measure of comfort.

The guardians raised their ghostly weapons in unison, their hollow voices echoing through the chamber.

"Prove your worth or perish."

The ground heaved, and from the earth rose several towering figures—golems, their bodies covered in the same ancient runes as the guardians. Kai unsheathed her sword and stepped backward.

"There's six of them," Liu said in disbelief.

Kai gripped her sword tighter, her eyes narrowing at the three golems that lumbered toward her. The other three went for Liu. The creatures gleamed with an unnatural green hue, and Kai suspected they were formed from jade. Their movements were slow but deliberate, and their weight caused the ground to shudder.

She considered how she might defeat them. Stone could be cracked, chipped, or broken, but jade—especially jade fused with magic—was a different challenge altogether.

Hikari's presence entered her mind. *They are not flesh and blood, but they have weaknesses. Find them, and you will bring them down.*

Kai wondered how the dragon knew what she faced, but she didn't have time to ask. The nearest golem raised its arm, the sound of creaking stone filling the air. It swung downward with terrifying speed, and Kai dove to the side just in time. The impact shook the ground, sending up a spray of dirt and shattered stone.

Liu was already on the move, his sword flashing in the dim light as he aimed for the joints of the golem closest to him. His blade met the jade with a metallic clang, but it barely left a scratch. He dodged a swing and back peddled.

"We need a strategy," he said.

Kai was back on her feet, her eyes flicking between the golems and the spectral guardians that now ringed the chamber. The runes etched onto the golems' jade surface emanated a soft shimmer, almost making the stone appear translucent.

"They are connected somehow," Kai said. "The golems and the spirits."

"What happens if you break that connection?"

Kai didn't know, but his question gave her an idea. One of the golems took a step toward her. She sprinted forward to meet it, slashing her sword at the glowing runes etched along its arm. Her sword sparked against the jade, and she felt the magic briefly flicker. That was it—the magic.

"Aim for the symbols," she shouted. "That's the key!"

Liu nodded, his face grim with focus. He darted past one golem, ducking beneath its heavy arm, and brought his blade down on the runes of its leg. The jade flared with a burst of light, and a deep crack appeared where his sword had struck.

"It's working," he said, dodging another swing. "We just need to—"

Before he could get the words out, another golem barreled forward, moving faster than its size suggested was possible. Its massive arm swung toward Liu, who barely had time to react. Kai's heart leaped into her throat as the blow connected, sending Liu flying backward. He crashed against the wall and slid to the ground, unconscious.

"Liu!"

Kai sprinted forward, her sword slicing through the air with precision. Her black blade connected with the largest rune on the first golem's chest, and a web of cracks spread across its torso. The golem faltered, its movements slowing as its magic began to unravel. That sent the others into a frenzy.

Ducking low, Kai ran to Liu's still form and stood in front of him. The golem Liu had struck drew closer, and Kai plunged her sword into the weak point he'd created in the creature's leg. With a loud crack, the limb shattered, sending the golem toppling to the ground with a deafening crash.

That left four still standing.

They wasted no time closing in. The guardians watched in silence, their gazes unwavering. Kai remained protectively in front of Liu's body, her mind racing for a plan to defeat the remaining golems.

Thinking about the cracks she had created in the first golem, Kai focused her attention on exploiting those weaknesses in the others. Ignoring the looming danger, she darted between the advancing golems, striking at their glowing runes. With each hit, cracks spiderwebbed across their jade bodies, the chamber echoing with every strike.

Kai fought with all the strength she could summon, but her energy was quickly fading. The weight of the situation pressed down on her, and she feared the end was near. Her breaths were labored and sweat made her clothes stick to her skin. She felt constricted, her movements growing sluggish.

She stumbled and fell, landing hard on the ground and her sword clattered as it bounced out of reach. Kai frantically searched for the magic that she had tapped into before, but it eluded her. The remaining golems advanced, and Kai saw her life flash before her eyes. She wanted to get up, to keep fighting, but her muscles felt like lead.

The massive creatures towered over her, and one of them raised its foot to crush her. Kai braced herself for the blow, but a battle cry startled her. She saw Liu on his feet, blood running down the side of his face from a wound on his head. He slammed his sword against the side of the golem about to step on

Kai, which threw the creature off balance. It fell to the ground, and the others turned their attention to him.

Kai forced herself up and crawled on all fours to get to her sword. She snatched the blade up and stood, turning just in time to see the golems converge on Liu.

"No!"

He crumpled under their blows and lay still. Kai's vision blurred, and her arms trembled. She reached inward, feeling for the threads of magic that bound her to Hikari. At first, they slipped through her grasp. It was like trying to catch water in her hands. With a guttural shout, she tried again, and this time she managed to grab hold of it.

A surge of raw power erupted from her. It slammed into the golems, pinning them against the wall. Their runes flared as if trying to resist her, but they burned away under her fury, the magic roaring like an untamed fire. The agony of watching Liu fall had unlocked something primal within her.

The wave of energy caused the spectral guardians to flicker like candle flames caught in a breeze. With a sharp cry, Kai directed everything at the golems. Their jade bodies splintered into a thousand pieces, creating a deadly storm of shards as the debris whipped about the chamber.

Kai released the magic and staggered over to Liu's body. She dropped to her knees beside him, her hands trembling as she checked for a pulse. It was faint and quickly fading. Dread washed over her. He was dying, and it was all her fault.

CHAPTER 15

"You have proven yourself worthy."

The guardian's words meant nothing. Tears blinded her, and she cursed herself for allowing Liu to come with her. If he'd have stayed behind with Kokoro...

You would be dead, Hikari said, her voice penetrating Kai's grief. *He sacrificed himself to save you.*

Kai wiped her tears away and looked at the guardian. It stood there impassively.

"Can you help him?" she asked.

"He is beyond all help."

Kai gasped and threw herself on top of Liu's body, tears falling freely. He had been more than a mentor to her, he had been her friend. Perhaps her only friend. Hikari's presence filled the bond, and a wave of comfort washed over her. It dulled the pain, but it didn't diminish it.

Time ceased to exist as she laid there. After a while, the tears stopped. She lifted her head to look for the guardians. They were gone, and in the center of the room stood a pedestal. Unfamiliar magic radiated from it, and Kai slowly stood. A shimmering mass of darkness sat atop the pedestal.

Kai approached cautiously, fearing there might be another test. She couldn't handle anything else. The cloak rippled like liquid night, its edges blurring and reforming in a mesmerizing pattern. Flecks of starlight danced across its surface, hinting at the vast power within its folds.

A conflicting mix of emotions churned within her. Kokoro said this cloak could help her defeat the Drakka, but at what cost? What would wielding such power do to her?

Power always comes with a price, Hikari told her. *But you have a pure heart and a just cause. If anyone can master it without being consumed, it's you.*

She sounded like Liu... the tears stung her eyes again, and she gritted her teeth against the pain. Pushing the agony aside, she grabbed the cloak. As soon as her fingers touched it, her eyes widened. The cloak seemed to be alive beneath her touch, its inky fabric undulating.

It's terrifying, she said.

Take it.

Kai lifted it from the pedestal. The weight of it surprised her. It felt both impossibly light and immeasurably heavy at the same time. With a fluid motion, she swung the cloak around her shoulders and drew it close. The moment it settled upon her, the world began to shift and blur. Darkness swirled at the edges of her vision, and she felt a peculiar sensation of being both present and elsewhere simultaneously.

Where did you go? Hikari's voice sounded distant, as if from underwater.

Kai struggled to focus, her perception constantly shifting between the physical world and something... other. Shadows danced around her, whispering secrets of ancient power and forgotten realms. She could sense the very fabric of reality bending and warping around her.

Hikari, can you hear me? It's overwhelming. I can see everything. The shadows, they're alive. And I can move through them, become one with them.

As she spoke, she felt herself slipping between realms, her body fading in and out of visibility. The boundaries where light and dark, physical and ethereal, blurred into meaninglessness. She was everywhere and nowhere, a being of shadow and substance.

This power is more than I could have imagined.

Control it, Hikari said, fear and awe mingling through the bond with her words. *You must control it.*

With a monumental effort of will, Kai forced herself to solidify, anchoring herself firmly in the physical realm. She squared her shoulders, and the cloak rippled around her like living darkness. She looked at Liu's body. The pain was still inside her, but it was distant now, as if many years had passed since his death.

"You deserve a better resting place than this," she said softly.

Kai lifted his body, cradling him in her arms. She thought he would be heavier, but perhaps she had grown stronger than she realized. Using the power of the cloak, she slipped into the shadow realm and walked through the walls, leaving the temple. She solidified and blinked against the harsh sunlight. Hikari regarded her curiously for a moment.

We will bury him at Tatenagawa, Kai said.

The dragon lowered her body so Kai could climb onto her back, and while still holding Liu's body, Kai heaved herself up, every muscle trembling. She situated herself and Hikari launched into the sky. The wind buffeted them, but Kai kept one hand tightly wrapped around Liu and the other held onto Hikari's scales.

How did you know what I faced in there? Kai asked.

We are bound as one. There were moments I could see through your eyes and hear what you heard.

Did you help me with any of the trials?

No, Hikari said solemnly. *I wanted to, but they forbade me.*

Who?

The guardians.

Kai sat in silence, her eyes tracing the shapes of Hikari's scales as she got lost in her thoughts. Liu had died to save her, and she would never forget that. With the Heart, and now the cloak, she would do whatever was necessary to bring an end to the Drakka.

The next two days seemed to last an eternity, but eventually, Tatenagawa grew visible in the distance, the temple rising like a dark sentinel against the horizon. Kai was relieved to see it, but she noticed smoke lazily curling into the air from one of the smaller courtyards.

Hikari roared and flapped her wings harder. Even from this distance, Kai knew the Drakka had returned. She prayed to her ancestors that Kokoro was safe, but something deep down told her the elder was in trouble.

As Hikari descended, Kai could see shattered statues and splintered gates. The temple grounds swarmed with Drakka, and there was no sign of Kokoro.

Do you sense her?

She is alive, but they have taken her captive. She says your sister is here.

CHAPTER 16

Kai's heart skipped a beat. Akuhara was here? Rage and disbelief warred within her as Hikari began her descent.

Land away from the temple, Kai said.

Hikari obliged, taking them down near the river. They landed with a thud, and Kai slid off Hikari's back, her knees buckling for a moment beneath the weight of Liu's body. He seemed heavier now, and his limbs had stiffened at odd angles. She gently laid him on the grass, brushing a stand of hair from his face.

Stay here. I will find Kokoro and return.

Hikari rumbled her displeasure. *I will come with you.*

No. I can use the cloak to get in unseen, but the Drakka will spot you easily. I will be back as quickly as I can.

They stared at one another for a moment before Hikari nuzzled Kai in the chest.

If anything happens to you, I will destroy everything in my path.

Tears came unbidden to Kai's eyes at the dragon's words. She had never felt a love as deep as she shared with the dragon. Blinking the tears away, she rubbed the scales on Hikari's snout and turned toward the temple.

Smoke clung to the structure's eaves, curling into the sky like a serpent. The once-sacred grounds were now defiled with the presence of the Drakka. Kai balled her hands into fists, the cloak shifting around her, responding to the rise of her anger. The temple was almost unrecognizable, looking more like a battlefield than a place of peace.

Pulling the cloak tighter around her, Kai faded from view, slipping into the shadows. Her body became one with the darkness, the sensation disorienting her briefly. The cloak seemed to guide her, and she moved through the ruins like a wraith, her form shifting between realms.

She found Kokoro in the heart of the temple. Her wrists were bound together with a heavy, shimmering cord that pulsed with dark energy. Her face was pale, her eyes half-lidded.

"Kokoro," Kai whispered, materializing beside her.

The elder's eyes fluttered open, recognition flashing across her face. "You found it."

"I did. What happened here?"

"I tried to fight them off, but they're too strong. Your sister…"

"Where is she?"

Before Kokoro could respond, a slow, deliberate clap echoed through the chamber. Kai whirled around, her heart pounding.

There, standing at the far end of the room, was Akuhara.

"Little sister! Have you come to swear your loyalty to me?"

Kai drew her sword and scowled at the woman. They might share the same blood, but Akuhara was no sister to her. She wore the same dark robes as she had at Ikje. Behind her stood two hulking Drakka, their eyes full of malice.

"What are you doing here?"

"I'm cleaning the filth," Akuhara said, glancing behind her at Kokoro, her upper lip curling with disdain.

"I won't let you harm her."

Akuhara chuckled darkly, a sound that sent a shiver down Kai's spine. "What do you plan to do? If you stand in my way, you will die."

"Why are you helping them? They want nothing but destruction."

"You're a fool. Our mother spoiled you and made you weak. I don't help them, I *lead* them. And at my direction, they will change the order of things. The empire will crumble, and in its place will be something new, something better. You can be a part of it… if you bend the knee. Swear your allegiance to me."

"I will not bow to you," Kai said. "Ever."

"Then you have chosen death."

Akuhara drew her blade, a curved katana that gleamed as though it was forged from silver. The two women circled each other, the air between them as taut as a bowstring. They rushed forward at the same time, the clash of steel ringing out like a struck gong.

Kai gritted her teeth and slid her blade along Akuhara's in a shower of sparks, pushing back with a grunt of effort. Her sister smiled, twirling away and flicking her wrist. Dark tendrils of energy spiraled from her fingertips toward Kai's face. Without hesitation, Kai brought her blade up and blocked them. Her sword ignited with a brilliant orange light, devouring the tendrils.

Akuhara hissed and unleashed another spell. Kai leaped back just in time. The ground where she'd been exploded into a shower of black energy, jagged cracks spreading across the temple floor. Kai could feel something flowing through the bond, an ancient wisdom from elders long past. She extended her hand and flames erupted around her arm. Jerking her arm forward, the fire soared through the air in a blazing crescent.

Akuhara dodged to the side, summoning a magical shield that took the brunt of the damage. What remained of it continued onward, striking the wall next to one of the Drakka. The brute didn't budge other than to snarl. Kai closed the distance, her sword a blur of motion. She brought it down in an arc, aiming for Akuhara's exposed side.

The woman twisted her body at the last second, parrying the strike, then sent a blast of dark magic that sent Kai backward, her boots skidding across the cracked tiles. She winced, her muscles aching from the impact, but she regained her stance. Pulling from their bond, Kai channeled the power into a protective ring of fire around herself.

In a blur of motion, Akuhara darted forward, her dark magic snuffing out the flames as she crossed the barrier, jabbing her sword at Kai's stomach. Kai parried the strike, but Akuhara suddenly changed direction, her blade coming dangerously close to Kai's throat.

Kai leaned back so far she almost toppled over, but she managed to keep her balance and avoid being struck. She could feel her sword begging for the blood of the Drakka, and the cloak wanted her to submit herself to the shadow realm. It was almost too much.

Hikari's presence filled her mind, giving her renewed strength. She pushed the distracting whispers of her weapons aside and screamed. Flames enveloped her sword again. She attacked Akuhara relentlessly, pushing her back with every strike, her fiery blade leaving trails of scorched air in its wake.

Her sister snarled, frustration scrunching her face. With a wave of her hand, she summoned a dome of swirling black energy. It expanded outward, forcing Kai to back peddle as the dome writhed and twisted.

Kai narrowed her eyes, gripping her sword tighter. She took a deep breath, centering herself. Then, with a sharp exhale, she focused the flames to the tip of her sword. In one swift motion, she lunged forward, her sword cutting through the air like a comet. The flames roared, a concentrated beam of fire that pierced through Akuhara's dome, shattering it.

The force rippled through the air, sending the two Drakka slamming against the temple walls and blasting a hole to the outside. Stone and timber debris flew in every direction. Kai pressed on, slashing and jabbing Akuhara into a retreat that took them outside. Akuhara tripped and fell flat on her back. Kai stood over her and extinguished the flames from her sword, then pressed the tip of her blade against her sister's throat.

"It's over," Kai huffed.

Akuhara's lips curled into a smirk. "You've already lost and don't even know it."

A roar split the sky, and Kai snapped her head up to the heavens. A massive shape hurtled toward the courtyard. It was the gray dragon from Ikje, the one bonded to Akuhara. The dragon landed with a sound like a mountain breaking, and the shockwave sent Kai staggering.

I'm coming! Hikari shouted.

Drakka poured around the dragon's bulk, rushing to the aid of their leader. Akuhara rolled away, and wave of intense heat washed over Kai as the gray dragon unleashed his flames. Her first instinct was to fall into the shadow realm, but the Heart of Flame called to her, insistent. She acknowledged the stone, and as the flames reached her, they parted on either side, leaving her unscathed.

Akuhara's eyes widened briefly, and Kai found satisfaction in her surprise. She pulled the heart out of her bag and palmed it, then gripped the hilt of her sword. With the heart, the cloak, and the ancient magic that flowed through the bond, she felt as if nothing could stop her.

With a cry that didn't sound like her voice, Kai unleashed everything she could summon. Fire, earth, wind, water, shadow—they all converged. The sky darkened and the wind howled, bending trees. The earth split and heaved, and a maelstrom of fire erupted from the fissure, its tongues licking the sky. Lightning bolts blasted down from the sky, striking the gray dragon repeatedly. He roared in anger and pain. Akuhara staggered back, looking to her injured dragon.

Drakka fell into the fissure, burnt to ash within seconds. Kai wanted everything to burn, and she forced more power into the mix. The courtyard fell away into oblivion. This was the power of a true dragon rider, the power of the elements themselves. It was the power to destroy all that existed... but also to protect it.

Kai regained control of herself and stopped the magic. The winds began to die, and the flames subsided. The earth sealed back up, leaving a mark that resembled a scar.

"Retreat!" Akuhara screamed.

The Drakka that remained didn't need to be told twice. They fled, their withdrawal a disorganized, chaotic mess. Akuhara climbed onto her dragon's back and he leaped into the air. His scales were blackened in several spots, and he flapped his wings awkwardly.

Akuhara stared at her with hatred, and the dragon turned and left.

CHAPTER 17

Kai's body cried out for rest, but she went inside the temple and knelt beside Kokoro. The elder was alive, but barely. Her breathing was shallow, and she looked as though she were fading quickly. Hikari's bulk blotted out the light as she stuck her head through the ruins of the temple wall.

"Kokoro, you're safe now," Kai whispered, her voice hoarse and fragile. "They're gone."

"You're stronger than I thought you'd be."

"This power is more than I can handle."

"You will learn," Kokoro replied, each word a labor of effort. "Speak the oaths."

Kai's brow furrowed in confusion. "What?"

"The... oaths..."

Kai realized what she meant, and she glanced at Hikari. *Do you know the words?*

They are inscribed in my blood.

Kai nodded and turned back to Kokoro. She brushed soot-stained hair from the elder's face, her touch tender, almost fearful, as if she were afraid to hurt her. Kokoro's eyes slid shut, and for a moment, Kai thought she was gone. Kokoro spoke again, but it was barely above a whisper.

"Hurry..."

"By the sacred flame and the ancient bond we share, I vow to uphold the honor of our ancestors, to protect our lands and its people with courage and wisdom. With my dragon as my guide and my strength, I pledge my life to the guardianship of our realm, now and for all eternity."

By the breath of fire and the skies we soar, I vow to honor our ancient bond, to protect our lands and its creatures with might and grace. With my rider as my heart and my spirit, I pledge my life to the guardianship of our realm, now and for all eternity.

"You... are no... longer... Chosen. You... are... Sworn."

A final breath escaped Kokoro's lips, and she went still. Kai wanted to cry, but no tears would come. There would be a time for them, she knew, but it was not now. She stood, her movements slow. Exhaustion threatened to overtake her, but she pushed through it. There was one more thing to be done before she could rest. She needed to bury her friends.

Hikari dug two deep graves, and Kai placed Liu's body in one and Kokoro's in the other. She stared at them for a long moment, not knowing what to say. There were no witnesses other than Hikari, but it felt wrong to say nothing. Eventually, she decided on her words.

"You have found peace from this world. I will hold you in my heart, grateful for the time we shared. Thank you for everything you taught me."

She nodded at Hikari, and the dragon filled the graves with dirt, using her claws to pack it down tightly.

Where do we go from here?

Kai turned her gaze to the horizon, in the direction Akuhara had fled.

We go to end this, once and for all.

TO BE CONTINUED IN...
SWORN

Did you enjoy this book?

If so, you'll probably like my others. You'll find a preview of some of my other works on the following pages.

Thank you for reading this one, and I hope you look forward to the next one!

A Preview of Trial by Sorcery

I marveled at the vastness of the Citadel.

It was home to the Dragon Guard, the greatest warriors of the kingdom. While that was impressive alone, it was made even more amazing because it was also the home of dragons. The massive, powerful creatures were kept in the lower chamber of the castle. At least, that's what my father used to tell me.

A wall forty feet high surrounded the city of Autumnwick, as well as the stone fortress that towered behind it. This was my first time seeing the place, and it was just as large and imposing as I'd always imagined it to be. The massive gates that provided entrance through the wall were manned with guards armed to the teeth. A small line had formed at the entrance as the guards checked everyone entering.

I traveled downhill and joined the line, adjusting my sword belt. The weight of the blade continuously pulled down on my pants. It made me reconsider my decision to use a side sheath instead of one that went over the shoulder. It was too late to change my mind now. I'd spent the last of my coins to reach the Citadel, and I doubted the school would allow me to carry a blade during my training anyway.

The line shuffled forward slowly. I did my best to remain patient, but it was difficult. I was finally here! The home of the Dragon Guard! I'd dreamed of joining their ranks for as long as I could remember. My father's stories had always been filled with awe and wonder as he described his dragon and the bond they shared.

Although it was still early in the day, the sky was clear and the sun beat down mercilessly. I could feel droplets of sweat running down my back and sides. I drank the last of the water in my canteen and continued to wait. After what felt like an eternity of baking in the sun, I was next for inspection. I glanced behind me and saw the line was much longer now. There were at least a hundred people waiting to get into the city.

"Hold it there, low born," one of the guards said.

I looked ahead, thinking he was speaking to me. He wasn't. His attention was on a girl in front of me with long black hair. They'd already given her sack a thorough check, but the one talking grabbed her by the elbow and pulled her aside. I couldn't hear what he was saying to her because he'd lowered his voice, but whatever it was, the girl did not look amused.

"You, stop gawking and get over here."

The other guard was glaring at me. I hurried forward. The guard looked me up and down and frowned.

"What's your business?" he asked.

"I'm here to sign up for the school," I answered, trying to ignore the sweat sliding down my back. The other guard was still speaking with the girl, and he was being a little too touchy in my opinion.

"Another low born seeking fame and riches, huh?"

The guard was wearing a helm, but the ends of his hair sticking out from under it were blond. He was a high born, a noble. They were all the same. They thought they were better than everyone else simply because they were born with a different shade of hair color. I'd been bullied in my hometown a few times, not just for my social standing, and I knew in a city this size that it would be much worse.

The problem with this guard, however, was that he was only paying attention to my hair. He clearly didn't notice the insignia that was sewn into my upper sleeve. I didn't like to flounce it, but sometimes it was fun to bring a noble down a peg or two.

"Stop it," the girl with the other guard shouted. He'd pulled her close and was trying to kiss her. I'd seen enough. I turned my body so that the guard could see my insignia and smiled at him. His eyes widened for a brief moment, then he collected himself and waved me through.

"Apologies," he muttered.

I nodded at him, still smiling, and walked over to where the other guard was harassing the girl.

"Is there a problem, cousin?" I asked.

Both the girl and the guard looked at me. The girl was confused and the guard looked irritated.

"I figured you would have been lost in the market by now," I said to the girl. I was hoping she would catch on to what I was doing and play along. She tilted her head ever so slightly as a wordless sign of thanks and stepped back from the guard.

"I'm fine," she huffed. "This gentleman was just telling me how to get to the school."

"How kind of you, sir," I said, showing off my insignia to him as well. He looked at it, then looked me in the eyes. He hated that he couldn't stop me. I could see the seething anger in his blue eyes.

"Would you mind repeating the directions? My cousin is terrible at remembering things like that. Aren't you, cousin?"

I exchanged glances with the girl. She shrugged. "What can I say? I'm not used to doing things on my own."

The guard glowered at me. Through clenched teeth, he said, "Go straight. Through the market. When you reach the wall, turn right. The entrance is on the left."

Before I could antagonize him further, he stomped past me and returned to his post with the other guard.

"A bit of a jerk, that one," I said. The girl was already through the gate, leaving me talking to myself. I followed her and had to walk twice as fast to catch up.

"I'm Eldwin," I said.

"Go away," the girl replied.

"I'm sorry, I thought I just helped you back there."

The girl stopped and turned around, placing her hands on her hips and giving me a death stare.

"Did I ask for your help?"

"No ..."

"Do I look like some sort of helpless wench that needs rescue?" she demanded.

"Uh, no ..."

"That's because I'm not," she growled. "I can take care of myself."

"Sorry," I said lamely, putting my hands up. Her eyes widened slightly at the sight of my right hand. "I didn't mean to upset you. I just thought ... never mind. Forget that I said or did anything."

I walked past her and continued following the road. The girl's response to seeing my mangled hand was the same as everyone else who saw it. Horror, disgust, you name it. It came as no surprise to me anymore.

The buildings on either side were short and squat, all of them built with a dull gray stone. The buildings on the right ended after several feet and opened into a large space filled with vendors. Multicolored tents were arranged in orderly rows and delicious scents filled the air, making my mouth water. My stomach growled and I absently patted it.

My breakfast had been filling, but I'd walked the last few miles to Autumnwick and now I was hungry. Considering I didn't have any money for food, I was hoping the school would provide meals. My father had never told me about his training days, so I wasn't sure what awaited me.

All the sights and smells temporarily distracted my mind from the girl, who I found to be quite pretty. Her attitude, on the other hand, made me question my judgment. I watched the various vendors as they stood under their tents, hawking their wares and trying to negotiate prices with potential customers. The sun seemed to grow hotter by the second as I stood there. I wiped the back of my hand across my forehead and was about to continue to the school when the girl walked up to me.

"I'm sorry," she huffed.

"Don't worry about it," I said.

"No, really. I didn't mean to be rude. It's just ..." she trailed off and looked down. "My whole life, people have tried to help me for their own gain. I've made it a point in my life to never need help from anyone."

What she said didn't make any sense. She was a low born like me, so what would anyone have to gain by helping her? I pushed the thought away.

"Apology accepted," I said. "I didn't mean to offend you or anything. I thought that guard was being a little forceful for his own good and thought I could help diffuse the situation."

"Thank you," she said. She paused a moment, then said, "I'm Maren."

Maren. That was different ... but beautiful.

"Nice to meet you, Maren," I said. "Are you really going to the school?"

"I am," Maren confirmed. "I want to be a Dragon Guard."

"So do I," I said. "My father was one."

"Was?"

"He died," I answered. "In a big battle ten years ago."

Maren's eyed widened. "Wait. Your father was Matthias Baines?"

I nodded. "That's how I got this," I pointed to the insignia on my sleeve. "Noble by Deed."

She stared at the patch intently for a moment, then turned toward the market. "Something smells good," she said. "Want to help me find what it is?"

I wanted to say yes, but because I didn't have any money, I was forced to decline. Thankfully, she didn't ask for a reason. I wouldn't have lied to her if she had, but I would have been embarrassed. My father's heroics may have earned my family a noble title, but that title didn't come with riches.

"I'll see you at the school," I said.

Maren shrugged and disappeared into the crowded marketplace. A droplet of sweat threatened to drip into my eye and I wiped it away, then continued toward the Citadel.

Girls were odd creatures.

A Preview of Scale of the Dragon

The sun glared overhead, reminding Mina why she dreaded Lord Klodian's summer hunting trips. He was almost obsessive in his desire to hunt dragons for sport, and he used Mina like a hound to sniff them out.

Her life hadn't always been so exciting. Once, she'd been a normal girl that worked the farm with her family … until they sold her to Lord Klodian. Those days seemed so long ago now. At least the memories no longer brought her to tears. She'd cried enough to last her the rest of her life, as far as she was concerned.

"Which way, girl?"

Mina's pace had slowed, prompting Lord Klodian's demand. She looked over her shoulder at him. He sat astride his black warhorse, his polished plate armor glinting in the sunlight. The visor of his helm was up, and he glared at her impatiently.

To his right rode a group of his retainers, and on his left was Vhan, Klodian's squire. The retainers stared at her with a bored expression plastered on their faces, but Vhan looked excited. The squire was always thrilled when it came to dragon hunts.

"This way," Mina replied.

She continued trudging along the dunes, following the subtle pull she felt from the scale embedded in her leg. It infuriated her that Klodian forced her to walk while he and his entourage got to ride horses. Certainly, he knew it would be quicker if she were mounted, but then again, he probably did it just to spite her.

Mina was Klodian's slave, and she knew it. Whether or not it was legal was another issue, but from what Mina had gathered so far in her young life, Dominion Lords did whatever pleased them so long as it didn't get them into trouble with the High Prince.

She supposed it was a small blessing to belong to Klodian. There were rumors that other Dominion Lords could be very abusive, violent even. While Klodian had never raised a hand toward her, he was manipulative and impetuous. Growing up amidst the wealthy and elite seemed to breed those qualities into people, though.

Ahead, Mina spotted a tall mesa that rose several hundred feet above the surrounding landscape. The top was flat, and the sides were steep and straight as if some underground creature had pushed it directly up out of the ground. The rock formation was various shades of red all intermingled, but that wasn't what caught Mina's attention.

It was the shadowed cave entrance.

She angled her steps toward the mountain and the scale in her leg began to burn. It was only slightly uncomfortable, but once they got within a few hundred feet of the dragon, the pain would be excruciating. It happened every time, but that never stopped her. It wasn't the fear that Klodian would punish her that kept her from turning away. It was her hatred for dragons.

They were the source of her misery. Or rather, one of them was. That didn't matter to Mina. The only good dragon was a dead one, and so she would continue to lead Lord Klodian on his hunts with the hope that—one day—he would kill the beast whose scale made her life a nightmare.

"It's there," Mina said. "Inside the cave."

"You're certain?" Klodian asked. "It's not on top, preparing to swoop down on us?"

She turned to regard him. Klodian hadn't kept his title as Dominion Lord for no reason. He'd been born to the position, certainly, but that didn't guarantee someone the title for life. There was always some young upstart who wanted the power and fame for themselves, and Klodian's quick wits and suspicion had saved him from many assassination attempts.

"I'm certain, my Lord. The scale may be a curse, but it never lies."

"One man's curse is another man's godsend. You may not like your ability, girl, but your gift has increased my wealth fourfold."

That was another thing that bothered Mina. Lord Klodian always referred to her as 'girl' and never by her actual name. She supposed he did that out of spite, as well.

"You are entitled to your opinion, as am I. And I say it is a curse."

Klodian laughed and slid off his mount, landing with a clatter as his plate mail jounced about. He unsheathed his sword from his waistbelt and quickly looked it over, then returned it. He motioned to Vhan, and the squire also dismounted. Vhan carried a spear, but the weapon wasn't his. He hadn't earned the privilege of learning to fight yet.

"Wait for me out here," Klodian ordered, taking the spear from Vhan. "I'll be back shortly."

Mina watched him disappear inside the cave. The retainers began talking amongst themselves, sharing gossip and discussing things that made Mina wish a dragon would swoop down on them. Whether it ate them or her didn't matter, so long as it put her out of her misery.

Vhan slowly sidled around to where Mina stood, a grin on his face.

"Don't even ask," Mina said.

"I've never seen it," Vhan replied. "And I *really* want to see it."

"Why? So you can make fun of me, too? No, thank you."

"I wouldn't make fun of you. I think having a dragon scale in your leg is neat. I'd have one if I could. How did you get that, anyway?"

"I'm sure you've heard the stories," Mina said.

"I've heard rumors, which is usually far from the truth. And I've never heard the story from you, so ..."

Vhan stared at her expectantly.

"I fell on it."

"Care to elaborate?"

Mina heaved a sigh, knowing Vhan would irritate her until she gave in.

"I was playing in the hills when I was young, and a hole opened up beneath me. I fell into a dragon's nest and landed on a pile of scales. This one," Mina slapped her thigh, "happened to penetrate my skin."

Vhan's eyes were wide. "Seriously? That must have been amazing. Being in a dragon's nest, I mean."

"The nest was abandoned. And it wasn't amazing at all. It ruined my life."

"You're alive, aren't you?" Vhan asked.

"I exist, but I wouldn't exactly call being a slave to Klodian living."

"Some people don't like him, but I do. He's always nice to me. I have a warm bed and food to eat, so I can't complain. There wasn't much to go around at my home, so being the squire to Lord Klodian has been the best thing that's happened to me."

Mina offered him a fake smile in the hopes that he'd get the hint and stop talking, but he kept yammering on about how great it was to be part of Klodian's Dominion. Mina tuned his voice out and watched the cave entrance, wondering how long it would take Klodian to kill the dragon. Her leg was still burning, which meant it wasn't dead yet. At least he hadn't forced them to go into the cave with him.

After a while, Vhan left her alone and wandered over to listen to the retainers. Mina rubbed her leg, massaging the skin around the edges of the scale. She didn't fear for Klodian's safety. If he died, then she'd have an opportunity to escape. It wasn't likely he'd be killed, though. Not when he had the power of his runes. That was another perk the wealthy nobles enjoyed: magic.

Rune magic was sanctioned by the High Prince, and it was only lawful for nobles to employ it. Everything else was outlawed, but that didn't stop people from practicing it in secret. Although Mina had never met any illegal sorcerers, she knew they were out there. It was whispered that on the fringes of the Dominions, there were people who openly sold their services to others.

The burning in Mina's leg ceased abruptly, and she smiled. Another dragon was dead. *Good riddance,* she thought. A moment later, Lord Klodian stepped out from the cave. He was covered in dust and blood, and he carried a severed horn in one hand. Vhan rushed over and fawned over him, ever the loyal squire. Mina found the display annoying and turned her gaze away, looking up at the mesa's jagged walls.

"That's the first dragon of the season," Vhan said.

"The first of many," Klodian replied. "Girl."

Mina looked at him, and he tossed the horn to her. She caught it and turned it over, examining it. It was small, and she guessed the dragon must have been an adolescent.

"For your collection," Klodian said.

"Thank you, my Lord."

"Ride back to the castle and summon the workers," Klodian instructed Vhan. "Tell them to bring plenty of wagons. The beast was hoarding enough trinkets to fund an army."

"Right away, sir."

Vhan got on his horse and rode off. The retainers gathered around Klodian and listened to him relay how he killed the dragon. Mina ran her fingers along the horn, feeling the coarse lines that grooved its surface. Every horn was different, but they all had similarities. She glanced at the cave and thought she saw glowing eyes staring back at her from the shadows. She blinked a few times and squinted, but there was nothing there.

It was probably her imagination. She waited for Klodian to finish bragging about his kill, and then they began the trek back to the castle. Mina clutched the horn in her hands, hoping that the next dragon to be killed would be the one to set her free.

How she hated dragons.

When rumors of a dragon attack reached Demetrius, he dismissed them almost immediately. Having lived in the port city of Radda his entire life, he had heard many wild stories from countless travelers. Everything ranging from giant squids in the open seas to horses with wings. Admittedly this *was* the first time he heard mention of a dragon, supposed giant mythical creatures that fed on the fear of people and could lay waste to entire cities.

"Rubbish," he said. "Children's tales told by parents to scare little ones into obedience."

"I believe it," the old sailor remarked enthusiastically. "Captain heard it 'imself. Says the whole city was burned to the ground and everyone killed."

"Then how did your captain hear of it?" Demetrius eyed his friend sternly. The man's face was covered in wrinkles and his hair bleached from constant sun. The man had been a sailor since he was not more than a boy and was prone to believe almost anything.

"What d'ya mean?" the sailor, Bannigan, asked.

"If everyone was killed, how did your captain hear this story? Who would have repeated it to him?"

The old man remained silent for a moment and scratched his prickly-haired chin. "It not be my place to question the Captain, silversmith."

Demetrius laughed heartily. "Nice cover up."

The sailor stomped his foot indignantly. "It ain't no cover up. I trust the Captain's word. How's business?" Bannigan changed the subject.

"Profitable, as always. The war with Oakvalor hasn't put a pinch in anyone's pockets yet. I hear some of my fellow smiths have been requested to appear before the king, as to why is anyone's guess."

"Maybe the king needs more weapons."

Demetrius shrugged his large shoulders. He wasn't in the business of making weapons, so it mattered little to him. His craft was typically sought after by the well-to-do, custom pieces that didn't come cheap. Some people had so much money they apparently didn't know what to do with it. He could work with any metal he put his hands on, but he preferred silver. It was very easy to bend and could be cast or hammered which allowed him to form almost anything with it; from teapots to statues.

The clanging of the bell tower echoed loudly across the city, signaling noon. The bell tower was originally built to alert the populace of emergencies. Its main use now was to indicate the time. Bannigan clapped Demetrius on the shoulder and bid him farewell. "That's my call," he said, trying to be heard over the noise. Demetrius' shop was situated near the docks for convenience and the daily clanging of the bell had eventually become a normal sound to him.

"Be safe," he called out as the old man left. Bannigan waved to acknowledge he heard him. Not that anyone couldn't.

Demetrius was a large man with a thunderous voice. At six and a half feet tall, he was a beast of a man, with muscles so large that he had to be custom fitted for his clothing. His hair was light brown and cut short to keep it out of his eyes, and to keep it from being singed. His skin was a deep bronze color as he preferred to be in the sun most of his time.

He watched his friend until he could no longer see him among the crowd. He heard his name a few stalls down and glanced to see who said it. He could see a member of the king's guard talking to one of the vendors. The vendor pointed towards where he was standing. What in the Divines would a soldier of the crown want with him? He watched the soldier approach.

"Demetrius?"

The big man eyed the soldier warily. "Yes?"

"The silversmith?" he asked with an air of impatience.

"Yes."

The soldier withdrew a scroll from his belt and handed it to Demetrius. "What's this?" he questioned. The soldier shook his head. "Not my business, sir. I am just the messenger. I believe His Highness requests your presence at the palace."

"What for?" Demetrius probed.

"Not my business." The soldier's impatience was evident by his short, almost rude, answers. "I must be on my way, sir." The soldier turned and headed back from the way he came. Demetrius stared at the scroll, unsure if he even wanted to open it. Everyone knew he didn't make weapons. Why would the king summon him if he was seeking smiths to make his armies more weapons?

He snapped the seal in half and opened the scroll. It read:

To Demetrius the silversmith,

Greetings from the Esteemed Ruler of Talvaard, King Garun. Your presence is requested at the palace. Do not worry about your business. You will be well compensated. A carriage has been arranged to meet you outside the city of Radda at sundown. Do not be late.

King Garun

There was a fancy signature and the crest of the king, a phoenix bursting forth from a pile of ashes, at the bottom of the parchment. Demetrius sighed. He hated politics.

Dusk found him standing near the road at the outskirts of his hometown. He had closed up his shop early much to his disappointment. There was a certain beautiful woman who walked by his stall everyday around the same time, usually carrying fresh bread. He had only noticed her because he caught her staring at him as she passed by one day.

Her look was one of admiration. At least, that's how he took it. She had smiled embarrassedly and blushed. And so Demetrius made it a point in his day to watch her as she walked by and smile at her.

Closing early meant that he missed her.

He was more than slightly frustrated by that, as he had finally worked up his nerve to actually speak to her. His hope was that she would let him get to know her and perhaps they would see where things went from there.

The carriage pulled up suddenly and Demetrius noticed that the sun was just sliding behind the mountains. "Well at least the king is punctual," he muttered beneath his breath. The door to the carriage swung open and a man dressed in plain clothes, probably a servant, stepped out. He motioned to the carriage and bowed low. "If you would, sir."

Demetrius dipped his head in thanks and climbed inside. A quiet whistle escaped his lips. The inside was adorned with all sorts of glittering shapes. He looked closely and recognized most of the precious stones. Diamonds and rubies comprised most of the decorations, but there were also a few sapphires and a couple stones he did not recognize. The fabric that made up the seats was comfortable and smooth to the touch. It was hard to tell whether the material was dark red or brown in the fading light.

Demetrius was impressed. He didn't expect to be brought to the palace in luxury. Granted he was known among the higher ups for his skills in crafting, but he was not of noble birth. And most, if not all of them, seemed to ignore the fact that he was much wealthier than most of them, anyway. The servant did not get back into the carriage, but instead shut the door and climbed into the seat with the driver.

He had a decent amount of time to think as the buggy headed toward Tarvaarin, the city built around the palace. It was a thirty-minute trip to the palace by horse. After what seemed like hours to him, he felt a difference in the road. Instead of bouncing about on the dirt path, the ride smoothed out and he could tell they were now on the stone paved roads of the city.

The carriage came to an abrupt stop and the door swung open. The servant stood there and motioned for Demetrius to come out. He had gotten comfortable and it took him a minute to move. Why did the king want him to come so late in the evening hours, he wondered.

The servant led him through enormously tall double doors and into a massive circular room that was normally filled with nobles and commoners alike, usually bringing petitions and requests to the king or his advisors. The room was empty and their footsteps reverberated off the walls.

Demetrius looked admiringly up at the vaulted ceiling, rising sixty feet above him. Support pillars were spaced every ten feet, outlining the main walkway through the antechamber. "This is huge," he remarked to himself.

"Sir?" the servant looked back at him. Demetrius shook his head and the servant continued his hurried pace. A door in the middle of the far wall was flanked on either side by two giant alabaster statues of winged men standing at attention, their swords drawn and held up before them. Demetrius thought them an odd addition to the room. The walls were covered with portraits of regal looking men, whom he assumed were previous kings, and large brightly colored tapestries depicting scenes of long ago battles.

He began to wonder why he had never made a trip to the palace, if for no other reason than to say he had been there. The servant stopped before the door. "Wait here, sir," he said breathlessly before disappearing through the door. Demetrius looked down at the floor. Stone tiles, painted orange and yellow, ran the length of the entire room, forming a triangular pattern. The tiles outside the three-sided shape were bright red.

He assumed there was some sort of significance to the design, but it was lost on him. Demetrius looked back up and noticed the servant was staring at him. "His Highness will see you now." He held the door open and pointed down a long hallway. "It's the last door on the left at the end of the hall."

The big man nodded his head in thanks and walked to where he was directed. The hallway, large enough to comfortably hold two carriages side by side, was barely adorned at all. A guard stepped out from the shadows and startled him. "I didn't see you," he laughed nervously.

"That would be the point," the guard answered, his face hidden by the hood over his head. He patted Demetrius down for weapons and finding none, opened the door for him to enter. "Go to the center of the room and do not leave the circle."

"Circle? Why not?"

"Just don't."

Demetrius was starting to regret having made the trip. Then again, seeing how guarded the king was, he doubted he would have lived long had he refused to come. He walked to the middle of the room and noticed the circle design in the floor. He assumed that's where he was supposed to stand.

The guard shut the door and Demetrius was enveloped in darkness. He cleared his throat and the sound echoed eerily. Torches flared to life and revealed a large wooden chair with a man seated on it.

"Demetrius," the unknown man greeted. "I don't think we've had the pleasure of meeting before."

Demetrius wasn't sure if it was the king or not. And if it was, should he bow? He didn't answer. The man must have took his lack of response as hesitance. "You can speak freely."

Demetrius felt a little better that he could speak his mind. He wasn't one to bite his tongue. "What is this about? Why am I here? I am a very busy man, and I have lost half a day's time—"

The man in the chair stood up swiftly and Demetrius fell silent. "I can assure you, master smith, that we are all busy. Some busy with tasks more important than others." The man tossed a leather pouch onto the floor in front of him. "Consider this payment for your time."

Demetrius didn't dare move from the circle to see what was inside, heeding the warning the guard had given him.

"Talvaard has a shadow cast over it, master smith. A shadow that threatens to consume us all."

Demetrius assumed the shadow was Oakvalor, the enemy kingdom that Talvaard had been at war with for as long as anyone could remember. "Then I must inform you, sir, that I am not a weapon smith. I make trinkets and items ordered for noble houses. I think you have erred in your selection of men to build your weapons of war."

"Do you think that I am ignorant of those in my kingdom?" the man asked, revealing that he was indeed the king. "I know what you are capable of, Demetrius, and I have not summoned you here to build weapons. At least, not in the sense that you are thinking."

"What do you mean?"

Several other torches lit up, as though by magic, and exposed King Garun in all his splendor. He was shorter than Demetrius by at least a foot. His hair was long and black, pulled back tight into a ponytail. His nose slanted down his face, reminding Demetrius of a bird's beak. His eyes were hazel and set deep in his head. The king was nothing special in terms of attractiveness. What he lacked in looks, however, was made up for in bearing.

His posture and demeanor exhibited a great deal of confidence and his general appearance was enhanced by his garments. His crown gleamed in the torchlight and gave the impression that it was made of silver. Demetrius knew it wasn't crafted of his favorite metal, but was instead made of something much more valuable: white gold.

It had three gems set in the front. A rare black diamond, twenty karats by Demetrius' estimate, in the middle, surrounded on either side by two green serendibite stones. It was a marvelous treasure. The king's shirt was turquoise and had a lustrous, dazzling sheen that only silk could give. His linen pants were a brilliant green color tucked into black leather boots. During the daylight hours, when dealing with matters of state, he would also wear a mantle that extended to the floor, joined at the neck and open down the front, that was emblazoned with the large phoenix crest on the back.

"I'm sure you have heard the rumors?"

"Of dragons, Your Highness?"

"Indeed. I can read the disbelief in your face. I know how you feel, as I too was of the same mind when word first reached me. I can assure you," the king's tone grew somber, "there is no myth to these tales."

Demetrius was dubious. "What in the name of the Divines are you talking about?

Dragons? Winged creatures that fly and breath fire? You can't be serious, Your Highness."

The king's face remained solemn. "Had I not seen the creature for myself, I would be as doubtful as you, Demetrius. Unfortunately," he paused, gave a great sigh, and continued, "it is very real."

Demetrius was still in doubt, but he didn't further voice his suspicion. "What does all this have to do with me?"

"It is said that no one in Talvaard can work silver like you."

Demetrius had certainly earned a strong reputation for himself, but he was down to earth and didn't like to boast. "So I have heard," he replied, shrugging his large shoulders. "You still haven't answered the question."

The king closed the distance between him and Demetrius with a few quick steps. "I cannot reveal the details just yet, as I myself do not have them. All I know is that the skills of a silversmith are required, along with a few other details. Our ally," he used the word frostily, "does not have the privilege of metal smiths. And we lack what they have. So you see, master smith, you would be doing Talvaard a great duty."

"And if I refuse?" Demetrius asked, more out of curiosity than rebelliousness. A job for the king could prove to be very profitable.

Garun eyed him dangerously. "It would not be in your best interest ... but you have a week to consider it."

Demetrius felt goose bumps run up his back under the king's baleful look. "I am loyal to my country, Your Highness. I would never refuse an opportunity to serve the crown."

Garun smiled, the first Demetrius had seen on his face, apparently pleased with the answer. "My servant will escort you out and deliver you back to your home."

"When will you require my services?"

"You will know," the king answered.

A Preview of Throne of Deceit

The Seven Stars inn was busier than normal.

That was good for business, but it also meant that Gwen had been rushing around most of the evening, filling tankards and delivering steaming food. It was warm, uncomfortably so, and Gwen was glad the night was almost over. The air was thick with pipe smoke and boisterous laughter, a rarity these days.

Gwen spotted a man waving his arm, tankard upside down on the table. She heaved a weary sigh and hurried to the table, forcing a smile.

"More ale?" she asked.

"Yes, and keep it flowing," the man replied.

Gwen could tell by the way he slurred his words that he'd probably already had too much, but she nodded and refilled his tankard. The inn would be closing soon, so not much more ale would be "flowing" anyway. Gwen's father had been in the kitchen since opening, fulfilling the endless stream of orders and cursing when he burned himself, which was quite often.

A bard began playing a cheerful song, his fingers flying over the strings of his lute with a practiced ease. Gwen liked the melodies he played, but he was passing through and tonight would be his last performance at the inn. She did another loop of the tables, making sure the patrons were taken care of, then sat behind the bar and listened to the music.

Gwen found the bard handsome. He was young and energetic, his face clean shaven, and his brown hair trimmed short and neat. Her father would never allow her to marry someone with a profession that required constant travel, but she didn't see any problem with admiring the man's attractiveness. Besides that, it was common knowledge that Gwen would take over the Seven Stars once her father retired.

As the bard finished his song, a commotion outside the inn caught Gwen's attention. She looked to the windows, but it was too dark to see anything other than vague shadows. The noise drew the attention of the inn's customers as well, and the people quickly congregated in front of the windows. Those who couldn't squeeze in among the others exited the doors to see things up close.

Gwen heard angry shouting and groaned. Drunken men fist fighting one another wasn't uncommon, especially when the place was busy. She removed her apron and hung it on one of the hooks on the wall, then walked to the door and cracked it open, peering out into the night.

A single man was surrounded by a group of the king's soldiers. Their black leather armor made them blend in with the darkness, but Gwen knew the attire. The soldiers had become a common sight around the inn, and around Dawsbury in general. Rumors of war had been circulating for years, but now there were signs of it. Aside from the presence of the king's men, there were also whispers of dark magic and sightings of dragons.

Gwen didn't know what to think about any of it. She lived a simple life working at the inn, and she wanted it to stay that way. The king could make war on the surrounding kingdoms if he wanted to, so long as Gwen's way of life wasn't impacted. Her attention was jerked back to the present when one of the soldiers kicked the back of the man's legs, knocking him to the ground. The man being harassed scowled and tried to get back up.

"Stay down, dog," one of the soldiers said.

"Yeah," chimed in another. "If you know what's good for you."

Someone bumped into Gwen from behind and she looked over her shoulder to see Tobias, the baker's son.

"What's going on out there?" he asked.

"Some of the soldiers have taken an interest in Garre," Gwen replied. "Garre's angry, but I think he'll keep his temper under control."

"I can't stand those soldiers," Tobias muttered. "They think they can come to our town and do whatever they want just because they wear the king's emblem."

"As long as we stay out of their way, we don't have anything to worry about," Gwen said. "They're just following orders."

Tobias snorted but didn't say anything.

Garre was glaring daggers at the soldiers, but he stayed where he was.

"Good dog," one of the soldiers goaded. "Now lick the dirt off my boots."

"Screw off," Garre spat.

The soldier who'd spoke drew his sword and leveled the tip at Garre's throat. "What was that, dog? Did I tell you to speak?"

Silence fell over everyone in the inn. Gwen watched intently, her heart hammering in her chest with anxiety. "They can't kill someone for no reason," she whispered.

"That's what you'd think, anyway," Tobias said. "When left unchecked, that tyrant's hired hands will do anything, including murdering innocent people."

"Watch your words, boy," one of the patrons said. "You'll bring the king's wrath down on us all."

Gwen watched with bated breath, silently praying that Garre wouldn't be hurt. She wasn't friends with him, but she knew who he was, and they'd never had any issues. Even if they had, Gwen would never wish harm on anyone.

"Get to licking," the soldier demanded, lifting his boot near Garre's face. For a moment, Gwen thought he was going to lick the soldier's boot. Instead, Garre grabbed onto the soldier's leg and pulled, forcing the soldier to fall onto his back.

"Yeah!" Tobias shouted. "Give him what for!"

Gwen had a feeling something terrible was about to happen. The soldier scrambled back onto his feet and kicked Garre in the face. Garre crumbled backward awkwardly, his legs tucked under his body.

"Gods," Gwen said, flinching and looking at Tobias.

"Someone has to do something," Tobias said. "They're going to kill him."

"Don't say that," Gwen replied.

Tobias stared at her, jaw clenched. "No more," he said.

Before Gwen could figure out what he meant, Tobias drew a dagger and pushed past her. He sprinted toward the soldier that had kicked Garre and leaped onto his back, driving the small blade into the soldier's chest.

The world froze.

Gwen's eyes widened in horror and surprise. She screamed, and the world began moving again, but now it was a blur. The other soldiers grabbed Tobias and forced him to the ground, wrenching his dagger away. The soldier he'd attempted to stab was uninjured.

"Some dogs don't understand loyalty," he said, then lifted his sword up threateningly. With a sudden grunt, he staggered forward as Garre pushed him from behind. Another soldier drew his sword and thrust it into Garre's back.

Gwen stepped back from the door, shaken. Garre screamed and fell to the ground, writhing in the dirt. There was confusion among the rest of the soldiers as they glanced at each other with uncertainty. Tobias broke free of the men holding him and sprinted to the left, running down the alley beside the inn.

The apparent leader threw his arms up. "Don't just stand there, get him!"

The others chased after Tobias and Gwen quietly shut the door and returned to the bar. The patrons slowly went back to their tables, but the mood had changed. The bard had stopped playing his music and the conversations became muted.

Gwen wrung her hands together nervously, not knowing what she could do to help Garre. Should she help him? What if he had done something to warrant the interest of the soldiers and she wasn't privy to that knowledge? She started to head around the bar when the kitchen door flung open and Tobias ran in, followed by Boris, Gwen's father.

"What's going on?" Boris demanded.

"I need somewhere to hide," Tobias replied. He looked around the inn, frantic. Gwen thought he looked like a frightened deer, ready to flee at any moment.

Boris looked around the room, noting the patrons, then grabbed onto the edge of the bar. "Help me, will you?"

Tobias grabbed the other end and, together, they heaved the stout wooden structure forward. Gwen was surprised to see a trap door hidden in the floor.

Boris opened the small door and motioned to the darkness within. "Go," he said. "Hurry."

Tobias didn't question the order and hurried down into the hidden space. Boris closed the door and tried to move the bar back into place, but it was too heavy. He looked at Gwen, then changed his mind and turned to the customers.

"Someone give me a hand!"

A few people leaped to their feet to help and, within a few moments, the bar was back in place.

"Father," Gwen said softly, following him into the kitchen. "You never told me about that door."

"Forget that you ever saw it," Boris replied, washing his hands off in a bucket of clean water. He went back to preparing meals as if nothing had happened.

Gwen watched her father work, wondering why his demeanor had changed so suddenly. There was something he wasn't telling her, that much was obvious. There was shouting in the common room and Gwen rushed out of the kitchen. The soldiers had entered the inn and were harassing the customers.

"Gentlemen," Gwen greeted loudly, offering the largest smile she could muster. "Drinks?"

"We're looking for a criminal," one of them said. Gwen turned her attention to him and recognized him as the leader of the group from outside.

"I don't think I've seen anyone shady in here, but I'll help if I can," Gwen said cheerily. She was surprised her voice hadn't cracked.

"This person is an enemy of the king. He's dangerous and we need to remove him from the streets. He's about my height and build, with black hair."

Gwen put a puzzled look on her face and slowly shook her head. "I can't say I've seen anyone like that in here. Would you like a drink while your men ask my customers?"

"I'd love one, but I must refuse. I'm on duty."

"Right. Can't have you out there staggering around on the job." Gwen laughed. The soldier didn't share her mirth. The kitchen door opened as Boris came out, carrying a tray full of food. The soldier jumped, obviously startled, then calmed when he saw there was no threat.

"Evening," Boris greeted as he passed them, delivering the food to a table by the windows.

"If you see anyone matching the description, please report it to the local constabulary. They'll get word to us."

"I will," Gwen replied.

The soldier turned his back to Gwen, and she noticed the uneasiness of the customers. Most were minding their own business, but a few people were staring death at the soldiers. Boris returned to the bar and the lead soldier stopped him.

"Are you the owner?"

"I am," Boris replied, offering a grin. "It's a humble place, but it's served me well."

"It's a dump," the soldier grunted. "I've also heard that it's a den of protection for the king's enemies."

Boris looked pained. "I hope no one questions my devotion to the king," he said. "I've been a staunch supporter all my years."

The soldier stared at Boris intently, then nodded, seeming satisfied.

"Anything?" the soldier asked his men.

"Nothing," someone answered.

"Let's go, then." The lead soldier looked from Boris to Gwen, then headed for the door. His men followed after him and they exited the inn. Gwen sighed in relief and leaned over the bar.

"That was close," she whispered.

There was a pounding noise at the door and Gwen realized that the soldiers were securing it so that no one could leave.

"Father, what's happening? Why did he say we're hiding enemies here?"

Boris suddenly looked older to her. Deep lines spread across his face and there were bags under his eyes.

"There are things I haven't told you because I wanted to keep you safe," Boris replied.

The customers of the inn began to panic and started kicking at the door. A few others picked up chairs and broke some of the windows, but they were greeted with flaming torches that were thrown into the inn. People scattered out of the way, knocking over tables and spilling drinks. Alcohol hit the torches and flames spread across the floor.

"We've got to get out of here!" Gwen shouted.

Boris grabbed her hand and led her through the kitchen to the backdoor, but when he pushed on it, it didn't budge.

"They've blocked us in," Boris said grimly.

"We're broke," Jayde said, casting a baleful glance at Lochlan, the ship's pilot.

"We'll find another job," Gavin replied. He was always defending Loch, and Jayde hated him for it. Perhaps hate was too strong a word. She turned her fiery gaze on Gavin and frowned. Fine, she didn't *hate* him. But it really annoyed her when he stood in the way of Loch taking responsibility for his mistakes.

"You know, we wouldn't have to find another job if Loch could stick to the plan and quit screwing anything that walks on two legs."

"That's not fair, Jayde, and you know it."

Loch stood up from his chair and crossed his arms. Jayde turned to face him, and they engaged in a silent stare-down. Her green eyes bored into his blue ones. Neither one would give in, and eventually, Gavin stepped between them and smiled at Jayde.

"Come on. We both know that Loch is never going to change, so we might as well accept the fact that he's going to screw us out of a few jobs."

"Yeah, literally," Jayde muttered. "I'll be in my bunk."

She stormed off to her personal quarters, wondering for the thousandth time why she continued to put up with Loch's constant stupidity. It was like he didn't use his brain sometimes and let his second head do all the thinking. They were so close to getting a huge payday, and yet again, Loch had ruined it. The lord of a small planet had hired them to clear out a gang that had taken up residence in his city. While the rest of the crew had been doing just that, Loch had snuck away with the lord's daughter.

A servant had caught them and immediately informed her master. If it wasn't for Jayde's quick-thinking and their even quicker escape, the lord would have executed them all. As it was, Jayde wasn't sure that they had gotten away without repercussion. The rear sensors on the ship hadn't detected pursuit, but that didn't mean they were home free just yet.

Jayde entered her personal quarters and shut the door behind her. She stared at her desk, debating on whether or not she should drink a small glass of Erillian wine. It always helped calm her anger. She was fuming. Loch had managed to really screw them over on this job. Their pockets were empty and her ship needed some work, not to mention they hadn't found a high paying job in months.

She sighed and walked over to the window and stared out at the stars. The vast black landscape stretched as far as she could see. The few stars that burned on the fringe of civilization sputtered and glowed dimly.

"Even the stars are dying out here," Jayde muttered aloud.

If they couldn't find a decent gig soon, she would be forced to land on some god-forsaken outpost until she could afford to refuel the ship. When she was young and wished to see the universe, she never thought it would be in a dilapidated ship with a crew of misfits. Hell, she never thought she'd be a mercenary either, but here she was. Captain Jayde Thrin of the *Determination*.

She snorted and turned from the window just as a massive jolt rocked the ship and pitched it roughly to the side. Everything on her desk slid off the smooth polished surface and crashed to the floor. The whole vessel groaned and Jayde thought she could hear an explosion in a distant part of the ship. She staggered into the hall, stepping over fallen items on her way out. The ship jolted again and she had to throw herself bodily against a wall to keep from tumbling to the floor.

The emergency siren blared overhead, followed by Loch calling her to the bridge. If he was calling for her, then there was a serious problem. He might be a worthless womanizer, but he was a damn good pilot. Jayde hurried down the hall to the bridge, barely pausing long enough for the doors to open.

"Blast it, what's going on in here—"

The words died on her lips as she surveyed the scene. Gavin was barely standing. He was holding onto a console, struggling to keep his balance. Loch was feverishly tapping buttons on the ship's control panel and cursing vehemently. The siren continued to blare loudly, and Jayde had all she could take.

"Turn that damn thing off!"

"I'm trying," Loch shouted. "We've been hit by something and our shields are down."

"Great! They haven't finished charging yet?"

"Not quite. They're at sixty percent." Loch tapped the screen with one finger. "Sixty-five," he corrected.

"That'll have to do," Jayde said. "Turn them on."

"Aye, Captain," Loch grunted.

A few seconds later, the ship began to hum as the shields kicked on. Loch managed to straighten the ship and Jayde sat in the chair beside him and checked the rear sensors. Not far behind them, a sleek Inquisitor ship was closing the distance. Jayde ground her teeth in anger and looked at Loch.

"Nice," she muttered. "Real nice."

Loch peered at the screen and his eyes widened in surprise. "To be fair, his daughter came onto me. I hadn't even noticed her until she—"

"I don't care," Jayde interrupted. "What's done is done. But if we survive, you'll be lucky if I don't turn you in to the Convocation and collect on your bounties."

Jayde smirked as Loch immediately stopped arguing with her. His warrants with the Convocation were a sore spot. Normally, Jayde wouldn't use that weapon against him, but she was furious with him for messing up this time. They desperately needed a payday. Now they weren't just broke, they were being hunted down by the local authorities.

"We're getting a communication request," Loch said.

"Put it through," Jayde replied.

She sat up straight in her chair. Loch tapped a button on the console and the large screen that hung awkwardly above the observation deck window flickered to life and the familiar face of Lord Rasking greeted them. Jayde groaned inwardly but put on a face of bravado.

"Lord Rasking," Jayde said.

"Mercenary scum," Rasking replied. "I find it so enjoyable that I found you with your pants down, so to speak. I'll make this easy for you. Let us board you without a fight and we'll kill you and your crew quickly."

Jayde laughed in response. "Come on, Rasking. This is the crew of the *Determination*. We don't do anything easy around here. I'll tell you what. Run with your tail tucked between your legs and I won't blast your hide to dust particles immediately. I'll give you a head start."

Rasking's face scrunched into a snarl. "The only one getting blasted to pieces is going to be you." He turned to someone offscreen and ordered them to fire. The *Determination* shuddered as a barrage of laser cannon fire blasted into the side of the ship. Jayde felt a slight tremor under her boots as the shields took the brunt of the attack. She slammed a fist onto the console, ending the video feed of Rasking's ugly smile.

"Shields down to forty-five percent!" Loch shouted.

"It's time to show this petulant lord who he's messing with," Jayde said. She pressed a button on the screen and leaned forward to speak into the microphone.

"McCready, get to the gunnery bay and return fire with the plasma turrets. I want that ship burnt to a crisp!"

Jayde hoped the old grizzled veteran wasn't asleep or passed out drunk. A few moments later, scattered bolts of light filled the sky and struck the Inquisitor ship head-on. The enemy ship's defenses glowed red under the assault.

Although the *Determination* was a cargo ship, it was equipped with the latest plasma cannons for self-defense. Jayde had learned long ago that space was, for lack of a better phrase, the wild frontier. Pirates roamed the black ocean of space, looting and pillaging anyone they came across.

"Gavin, get down there and assist McCready. If we can't get a hit on their ship, we're going to be in serious trouble."

The ship's navigator sprinted off to obey and Jayde turned her attention to the console. The shields were close to failing and their fuel was running low. She knew they had enough to possibly get them to a recharge outpost, but it wouldn't be very far from their current position. Unless they were able to maim the Inquisitor vessel, it wouldn't be much of an escape.

A second volley of laser blasts left the *Determination* and struck Lord Rasking's ship. McCready's deep laughter came roaring through the comms speaker.

"We're about to have an opening in their defenses," the veteran said. "I'm going to light him up!"

Jayde had a sudden trepidation about possibly injuring Lord Rasking. He was a member of the Convocation, after all. The fact that he had threatened to kill her and her crew, however, gave her the boost she needed to push that fear away.

"Take it when you see it," she ordered.

"Is that the best idea?" Loch asked.

Jayde ignored him. He had some nerve asking a question like that. Why hadn't he asked himself that before gallivanting with Rasking's daughter? *Bastard,* she thought.

"Call the engine room," Jayde said.

Loch did as she requested. There was a short delay, then Klaus's voice crackled through the speaker.

"I've got some issues down here. Can I get back to you?"

There was a noise that sounded like an explosion, followed by some incoherent shouts, then the audio cut off. Jayde glanced at Loch. Her face remained impassive, but she was sure he could see the uncertainty in her eyes. She gave Loch a slight nod to let him know she had everything under control, then turned to look out the window and spotted Raking's vessel turning in an attempt to flee.

"I don't think so," she muttered. "McCready, hit that ship with everything you've got."

A rain of plasma blasts fell onto the Inquisitor ship, causing multiple explosions to erupt along the vessel. Jayde watched with grim satisfaction as Raking's ship lit up with flames. And then it exploded, sending debris flying in every direction. A shower of metal shrapnel struck the Determination's shield and bounced off, floating lazily through space.

The sudden realization that they had just killed a member of the Convocation made Jayde's stomach drop. Loch wouldn't be the only one with warrants now.

"Get us out of here," she ordered Loch. "Now."

"On it," he answered.

Jayde left the chair and headed for the lift. She needed to see what the commotion was in the engine room. It was a welcome distraction from the fear.

"What was I thinking?" she berated herself. "Now Rasking is dead and I'm screwed. We're all screwed."

The lift came to a stop and Jayde could smell smoke. She hurried down the hall and practically leaped down the short stairwell into the engine room. Now she didn't just smell smoke, she saw it. Black clouds were billowing off one of the engines. Klaus stood nearby, spraying foam onto the flames. The ship's mechanic managed to kill the fire, but Jayde could see the damage was done.

"What happened?" she asked.

Klaus whirled to face her. "You scared the hell out of me! Announce yourself next time, will you?"

"Will do," Jayde replied. "Sorry."

Klaus shook his head and set the fire extinguisher down. He tilted his head to either side, stretching his neck muscles.

"Something hit us hard, which caused a load of debris to land on the engine. I tried to remove it, but the weight of it all crushed the casing and broke the engine wall. We're lucky it didn't simply explode and destroy the entire ship."

"That's good news," Jayde said. "Is it fixable?"

"Not with what we've got onboard. We need to stop somewhere. The other engine wasn't damaged, but it's not going to be able to power the entire ship."

"Great. Let me know if anything changes down here."

Klaus grunted in reply and Jayde went back to the lift. Their already bad situation had just gotten worse.

About the Author

Richard Fierce is a dynamic voice in the realm of fantasy, weaving tales that transport readers to worlds beyond imagination. His journey as a wordsmith began in childhood, but it was in 2007 that he took the plunge into the world of publishing. Since then, Richard has enchanted readers with multiple novels and short stories, showcasing his versatility and creativity.

In the year 2000, Richard Fierce earned the esteemed title of Poet of the Year for his captivating poem, "The Darkness." This early recognition hinted at the depth and artistry that would define his future literary endeavors.

Beyond the written word, Richard is a co-founder of the Acworth Book Festival, a significant literary event held in Acworth, Georgia. This initiative reflects his commitment to fostering a vibrant literary community and celebrating the written word.

A resilient spirit, Richard transitioned from a career in retail to the dynamic tech industry, finding new inspiration and challenges in the world of technology when he's not immersed in crafting fantastical tales.

In his personal life, Richard is a family man, navigating the joys and challenges of marriage and parenting. With three step-daughters (pray for him), three grandchildren, a menagerie of four dogs (his beloved huskies!), and a ferret, his home is a lively haven that resembles a bustling zoo.

Richard's enduring love for fantasy was sparked in high school when a friend's mother gifted him a copy of *Dragons of Spring Dawning* by Margaret Weis and Tracy Hickman.

This transformative experience ignited a passion that has since shaped his literary career, inspiring him to create worlds where dragons soar, and adventures unfold. As readers delve into Richard Fierce's works, they embark on thrilling journeys through the fantastical landscapes born of his vivid imagination.